Tales From Homer

By Conley Stone McAnally

SECOND EDITION

PHARAOH PUBLISHING USA

Also by Conley Stone McAnally

Tales From the Lake
Wilson Bay: Tales From an Eskimo Village
Jump, Alaska: Tales From the Interior
O'Brian's Black & Tan: Tales From an Irish Pub

TALES FROM HOMER
By Conley Stone McAnally

Second Edition, 2014
PHA009 • ISBN 978-0692300527

Pharaoh Publishing USA
www.pharaohpublishingusa.com

Cover art used under license

Produced and designed by Seann McAnally

Dedicated to Seann, Shannon, Darren, Meghan, and Kim.

Thanks for being here.

Contents

Prologue 7

Barn Burner 11

The Doodenville Men's Club 23

The Ballad of Clarence and Sally 33

Everybody Loves a Winner 41

Ezra Brown 53

Swamp Gas 56

Old Horse, or the Story of Jimmy and Betty 64

The Pride of Doodenville Flying High 75

Epilogue 86

Who's Who in Doodenville 89

Prologue

Several years ago I enrolled in a new sort of archaeology class at what is now my alma mater. The class was mostly field work, and it was different in the respect that we were not looking for dinosaur bones or Native American relics or the priceless artifacts that Indiana Jones and his ilk seek (although I did buy a fedora). No, this was what Professor Simpson called "village archaeology."

The prof had located a site in central Missouri not far from campus that he felt was just right for his fledgling class of wannabe archeologists. Our mission was to comb a square mile area among the ruins of an old village and find out what we could about the former inhabitants, to see if we could determine the "flavor of the times," as he called it. Most of the class found something: little glass vials, old hammers, wagon parts, ice tongs, scattered horseshoes, and even part of a vintage airplane. I, on the other hand, found nothing. Nothing, that is, until one day when I visited my grandfather in the old folk's home. I mentioned my recent college adventure and what miserable luck I was having finding anything of importance.

"You ain't looking in the right place," he told me.

"No kidding," was my reply.

He leaned forward in his chair. "Now, where is this place again?"

I gave him the general location and he nodded knowingly.

"Well, I know all about that place. Got wiped out by a tornado years ago and the damage was so complete they never rebuilt. Folks just went other places. Later, if you remember your history, they also had a big earthquake in these parts and it just flattened what was left there, which wasn't much. In fact a friend of mine used to be what you'd call the chronicler of the place, sort of the town historian, reporter, and poet laureate. He was also the city jailer."

"Gee", I said. "He would have been a great guy to talk to."

"Well, why don't you? He lives just down the hall".

Mr. Homer I Storebeck was old—a lot older than Grandpa—but how old I was never really able to determine. He was more than happy to discuss the old days and the history that surrounded the village. While my classmates were exploring and digging in the July heat, I wiled away my time drinking iced tea and listening to his yarns in the air-conditioned retirement home. This was far more palatable to my archaeological taste.

After several days of note-taking and recording, Homer asked me what I was going to do with all the information he was giving me. I told him I was going to compile the information into a term paper and present it to Professor Simpson and hope I got an A for the course.

He asked if original documents would help me out. I perked up because I had always heard that original documents or primary sources were much better than second hand accounts or broken pieces of pottery.

He then reached into an old trunk and pulled out a bunch of papers. "Think these might help?"

To: Dr. J. Simpson
From: C. Stone McAnally
Subject: Final Report on Village Dig 639

The attached report is based on interviews, original documentation, and prime source material. Some of the information helps validate field finds and interpretations of site research. I have used a rural narrative form and not the academic MLS format so as not to lose the flavor of the period.

CHAPTER 1

Barn Burner

BARN BURNERS ARRESTED!

C.W. Flowers

Editor, Publisher, Reporter

Doodenville—Yesterday, three men were taken into custody by the sheriff for setting fire to Steve Branson's barn. Steve Branson, the farmer who owns the barn (or what is left of it) should not be confused with Steve Branson the County Engineer. They are second cousins, however.

Ezra Brown, Samuel Horn, and Zeak Thurman were arrested for allegedly setting fire to the barn after Mr. Branson, the Engineer, said he saw all three men drinking and acting peculiar near his second cousin's place next to Lake River.

According to Sheriff Lenzi, all three men have refused comment, but Ezra Brown told this reporter that he is innocent and will tell all he knows at the court trial which is scheduled next week here in Doodenville.

The three men are being held in the Doodenville City Jail without bond because they don't have any money anyway.

Steve Branson (the farmer) told this reporter earlier today, "I hope the boys didn't do it. I've known them all their lives. I'd hate to think they'd treat me like this. Why, I've even had business dealings with Ezra."

As usual, soft drinks and candied apples will be provided prior to the trial.

Official Court Transcript:

Bailiff: All rise. Here ye, hear ye, hear ye. This court is now in session. The Honorable James Johns presiding.

Judge: Take your seats. Bailiff, the docket, please.

Bailiff: The County versus Ezra Brown, Samuel Horn, and Zeak Thurman.

Judge: Read the charges, Bailiff.

Bailiff: On July 21 of this year, ones Ezra Brown, Samuel Horn and Zeak Thurman maliciously and wilfully set fire to Steve Branson's barn.

Judge: For the record, which Steve Branson?

Bailiff: The farmer, your honor, not the engineer, but they are...

Judge: Yes, yes, I know, they are second cousins.

Bailiff: For the record, sir.

Judge: Yes, for the record. Do you boys have anything to say for yourselves?

Defendants: Yes, yes, yes. (Order of response unknown-cr)

Judge: Are you boys represented by counsel?

Ezra: By what?

Judge: By counsel, a lawyer. Do you have a lawyer to plead your case?"

Defendants: No! (In unison – cr)

Judge: Do you want one?

Samuel: Judge, we decided that we would have Ezra here speak for us.

Judge: Well, this is mighty unusual. I assume it is all right with you, Samuel. How about you, Zeak? Zeak?

Zeak: I...I guess so.

(noise in the back of the court room – cr)

Judge: What in tarnation? What's going on back there? Order in the court!

Crazy Jimmy Twofoot: It's just me, your honor. I dropped my tray of caramel apples.

Judge: Sheriff, get him out of here along with his caramel apples. I won't stand for these disruptions. This court will be conducted with dignity, even if I have to come out there and whip somebody. Now how do you boys plead? Guilty or not guilty?

Ezra: We don't know, Judge.

Judge: What do you mean you don't know? You know if you did it or not. If you did, you are guilty and if you didn't you are not guilty. Guilty or not guilty, what is your plea?

Ezra: Yes, I mean, we know if we did or didn't, but we don't know if we are or aren't. We don't know nothing about the...I guess you could say, the law. Can we, or me, I guess, just tell you what happened and then let you decide if we did, or didn't, or are or aren't? We know you are a fair and honest man.

Judge: Uh, well yes, why yes, most certainly. This is a little irregular, but yes, yes, my boy, go ahead, now take your time, just relax.

Ezra: Well, Judge, we was just doing a little drinking down around Lake River near Crisp Water Landing. As usual, Samuel Horn here got all drunkard up but instead of passing out or running along over to the Doodenville City Jail, he started dancing and whooping it up just like Crazy Jimmy does every so often.

Judge: Is what Ezra says the truth, Samuel?

Samuel: I reckon.

Judge: What do you mean, you reckon? Did you or did you not behave in a manner consistent with the testimony so far presented by Mr. Brown?

Samuel: I reckon I understand what you just said and I reckon I did what Ezra says I did but I was drunk and don't remember.

Judge: Has Ezra related the story correctly so far, Zeak?

Zeak: I …I guess.

Judge: I guess?

Zeak: I mean, yes, that's what happened.

Judge: Well, then let's see if I have this correct up to now. Samuel is acting crazy because of the alcohol, then what?

Ezra: Well, he, Samuel, starts running for Steve Branson's place and…

Judge: Excuse me for a moment, Ezra. Mr. Flowers, for the record have the court report indicate that this is Steve Branson, the farmer, not the engineer. Excuse me again, Ezra, you may continue.

Ezra: They are second cousins you know, Judge.

Judge: Yes, yes, I know. Now get on with it, Ezra.

Ezra: Well, like I was saying, Samuel goes running

toward Branson's place, his barn to be exact, and he runs inside the barn and closes the door. He must have locked it because Zeak and I kept yelling for Samuel to come out but it didn't do no good. That's when we noticed smoke coming out from under the door. Well, we did what does not come naturally when there is a fire type situation. Instead of running in a panic, we stood our ground. We yelled and kept hollering and trying to break down the door to rescue poor Samuel, and of course, put out the fire.

Judge: Well, you must have succeeded in rescuing Samuel. He's here.

Ezra: Well, not really. I mean, Samuel just opened the door and walked out.

Judge: You then tried to put out the fire with apparently no success?

Ezra: No, this time we did do what came naturally. We ran.

Judge: Then?

Ezra: Well, after we reached Crisp Water Landing, Samuel got this strange kind of smile on his face and started laughing like J.T. Williams did right before they hauled him off to that place up north.

Judge: Yes, sad, that was very sad. Then?

Ezra: He laughed for a while, then he cried for awhile. Then he noticed the jugs Zeak and I had left behind when we went off chasing Samuel. He grabbed them in his arms started running toward the burning barn and threw the jugs into the flames and all the time shouting "demon rum, demon rum!"

Judge: That is strange, real strange.

Ezra: It sure was, Judge, we weren't even drinking

rum.

Judge: Hmm. Do you concur with Ezra, Zeak?

Zeak: Do I what?

Judge: Concur. Did Ezra tell the truth?

Zeak: (inaudible reply – cr)

Judge: I didn't hear you Zeak. What?

Zeak: Yes, yes!

Judge: Okay, okay, Zeak, no need to yell. Samuel, what do you have to say for yourself?

Samuel: Not much. Nothing really. Gee, your honor, I don't remember nothing except waking up on the riverbank with the Sheriff standing over me.

Judge: Riverbank?

Ezra: Yeah, I mean, yes, Judge. After Samuel yelled about demon rum a few times, he ran back to the riverbank and passed out.

Judge: Samuel, I understand from Homer, the city jailer, that you spend a lot of time there.

Samuel: Well, yes, I do your honor. It's sort of like home.

Judge: Well, I'm going to see to it you become a real homebody. You are a disgrace to every drinking man in the county. I know you have had problems in the past, but so has everyone else. Every man is, or a least should be made to be, responsible for his actions. This is not the first time you have been in this courtroom because of something you did while under the influence. I am going to make a example of you, Mr. Horn (clearing throat- cr). I sentence you to ....

Zeak: No!

Judge: No? No, what?

Ezra: Shut up, you fool!

Judge: What?!

Ezra: Not you, Judge, I mean the other fool!

Judge: What? Hey, Ezra, get your hands off Zeak's throat!

Bailiff: Hey, you guys break it up! Sheriff, help me!

Ezra: I'm gona kill you!

Zeak: (making choking sound – cr)

Bailiff: Judge, grab his feet, Sheriff get one arm there, I got his neck.

Judge: Look out! (crash – cr) There, now get a rope. Sheriff, tie this man up. There now, order in the court. What in blue blazes is this all about, Thurman? Wait until I get behind the bench … okay, now go ahead. What is this all about?

Ezra: You dirty, rotten feather-headed skunk! I'll kill you!

Judge: Sheriff, gag that man.

Zeak: (in a shaky voice –cr) Brown is a no good deceiving liar. He don't know how to tell the truth. I was going along but I just couldn't let one man pay for what another done.

Judge: Well then, tell me what happened!

Zeak: Ezra's right about Samuel getting drunk. But he didn't burn no barn. Ezra done it. After Samuel passed out, Ezra and I kept drinking and, of course, talking. The more we drank, the drunker we got and the more we talked about things that we probably wouldn't have talked about. I asked Ezra about the horse he bought from Branson (farmer –cr) and Ezra went into a rage. He said that the horse was a no good plug and he had been cheated, and to top things off the horse had died and so on and so on. He really got madder and madder. The madder he got, the more he drank, and the more he drank, the drunker he got and the drunker he got, the more he talked and the more he talked and the more he talked the madder he got and the madder he got…

Judge: I think I get the picture.

Ezra: Well, then, he goes to feeling sorry for himself. I tried to tell him that Branson wouldn't cheat nobody on purpose, but he was way beyond listening to reason. He said it were folks like Branson that had made his life bad. He said everyone in the county has always been against him because he did not have a father anyone ever knew about. He said he was the only one in the county that people whispered about because of a situation like that. Then he drank some more and the more he drank the sorrier he felt for himself and the sorrier he felt for himself the madder he got at Branson. Then all of a sudden, Ezra said with a strange look on his face that he was going to show everybody and do the most terrible thing imaginable to Branson. I told him to do what he wanted, I didn't care. You see, I thought Ezra was just talking. I do remember telling him, though, not to burn Branson's barn. That would be inhuman. No man burns another man's barn, not for whatever reason.

Judge: But he did burn the barn anyway, right?

Zeak: Oh yes, and it was all my fault. He said he hadn't thought of that until I suggested it, and besides, he made me give him my matches.

Judge: Did you help him?

Zeak: No!

Judge: Did you try to stop him?

Zeak: I told him it would be inhuman.

Judge: But did you physically try to stop him?

Zeak: No. I just sat on the river bank next to Samuel.

Judge: So, I take it that Ezra, after burning the barn, returns to where you were waiting and then did what?

Zeak: Nothing at first. He just stared at the river for a long time and then at Samuel there passed out and all. Then he turned to me and said how I should have tried to help him stop Samuel from burning down the barn. He told me not to worry none though, because he would tell how I had helped him even though I hadn't, stopped Samuel, that is.

Judge: Now wait. Are you saying that Ezra burnt the barn, then decided to make it look like poor old drunk Samuel did it and tried to blackmail you into saying Samuel did it? Why did you go along with the story?

Zeak: I was afraid you would believe Ezra and not me, and I was sort of scared of Ezra. He can get violent, you know.

Judge: Take the gag off Ezra, Sheriff. Let's see what he has to say.

Ezra: Pig! Liar! Blast you all! Okay, I did it. Branson deserved it, the whole county deserved it, I'll burn the whole county down! I—

Judge: Order! Order in the court!

Ezra: (obscenity – cr) I'll burn the whole court down! You (obscenity – cr) have been against me all my life! All my life, even since my dear ole mother had me and never said who my Papa was, and didn't leave town. Wouldn't go to one of those places. You, you, and you are to blame. I'll kill my pop when I find out, it might have been you, or you, or you! I'll start with killing Zeak! (Noise, lunging, kicking screaming – cr)

Judge: Order, I demand order! Gag him again. There! Good, finally. This court will be conducted with dignity. Zeak, stop crying. I can't conduct a trial in this atmosphere. Court is recessed for fifteen minutes.

(Fifteen minutes later – cr)

Bailiff: All rise. Court is now in session again.

Judge: All right, be seated. Bailiff, are the three defendants ready for sentencing?

Bailiff: They are, your honor.

Judge: Samuel, you go home and I never want to see you back in this courtroom under any condition that might result from the use of alcohol. Zeak, you get yourself over to Steven Branson's house—the farmer—and help him rebuild his barn and anything else he needs help with for one month. Now, for you Ezra: no matter how bad a person's past has been, or no matter how many hardships he has endured, each and everyone must be responsible for his own actions. No amount of blame and no amount of accusing can take away the God-given right and duty of each of us to behave in a manner that is acceptable in a polite and civilized society. You have proven to this court—more than once, I might add—that you are deceitful, cannot be trusted, and a liar. It is my duty to remove you from our society in this beloved county once and for all. I hereby sentence you to one year in the Doodenville City Jail, and after release I think it would be to everyone's benefit for you to leave this county. It is hoped that by paying your debt to society and embarking on a new life, you may find it within you to start anew. Sheriff, escort this…barn burner…to the City Jail. Court dismissed.

Bailiff: All rise.

Officially Submitted: C.W. Flowers, Court Reporter (cr)

Homer I Storebeck
Doodenville

P.T. Sanders
Editor, The Atlantic

Dear Mr. Storebeck,

We enjoyed reading your story about the men's club you have there in Doodenville. However, at the present time it does not fit our editorial needs.

Thank you for your interest in The Atlantic and feel free to send other submissions. We will file this story and others you might submit in our Pull Pending Historical File and perhaps someday, we will publish them. We will contact you by letter, however, prior to publication.

Yours Truly,

P.T. Sanders

CHAPTER II

The Doodenville Men's Club

Final Draft as submitted to The Atlantic
By Homer I Storebeck

They don't talk about who has the best dog in town anymore. No sir, not since last December.

It was the middle of winter, and cold. Gosh it was cold! And snow—I mean you couldn't see from the window of Jessie Miller's General Store to the other end of the wooden planks that make up our sidewalks here in Doodenville. Everybody's always said it was the worst snow storm ever to have hit these parts.

Even though it was plumb miserable out, we all showed up about the same time we always showed up at Jessie's place. We had what you might consider a men's club. We didn't call it that, but every Saturday about sundown, or perhaps a little later, Steve Branson, Digger Johnson, Judge Johns and myself would get together and play checkers, tell stories, and more or less just brag to one another—which some might say was stretching the truth.

This one December evening, the bragging turned to our dogs. No man in Doodenville went anywhere without his dog. A man is judged to some degree on what kind of dog he has, and how he treats it and it him. Of course, everyone can't see how one is treating his dog all the time, nor it him, so we felt like it was our duty that winter night to tell one another. That is where the others always get into trouble, because they exaggerate a mite and this night they exaggerated a lot. Not me, of course.

The checkers match ended, and we began to sip a little of the stuff behind the counter that Jessie keeps for purely medicinal purposes—snake bites and such. Jessie was always there, but he seldom joined in because he was too busy keeping track of how much we were sipping and eating from the cracker barrel. Anyway, we were doing what we always did when Steve Branson popped up and said during a lull in the conversation:

"Now we've been talking about our dogs for nigh on three hours and Lord knows how many nights we've been doing the same. Let's settle it once and for all—who's got the best dog?"

Everybody seemed to think it was a pretty good idea, because each man thought he had the best dog and would win any such contest. We all thought a little and tried to come up with some sort of criteria that could determine a winner.

Steven Branson suggested that we could have them run a race, but that was scuttled because there was too much snow on the ground and it was too cold. "And besides," Digger Johnson said, "being fast don't mean nothing anyway."

He was right, of course. We all knew that Crazy Jimmy Twofoot's oldest boy, Jimmy J, was the fastest thing on two legs in three counties and the boy couldn't find his way to the outhouse without someone helping him. At least that's what Crazy Jimmy always said.

Then Steve came up with another idea (he was always coming up with ideas, being an engineer and all). He suggested that we have the dogs bark real loud and whoever's dog barked the longest and loudest would be declared the winner (I didn't say all his ideas were good).

Good or bad, that idea was ignored, because everyone knew Jessie's wife was sick with the virus and noise would wake her and cause some discomfort. Steve must have gotten the point also, because he snapped his fingers like something had just occurred to him and mumbled, "oh, yeah!" and sat back down. It seemed as though in all the years that I had known Steve he was always snapping his fingers about something.

We all sat around the stove and thought some more. Then Judge Johns cleared his throat. Now when a man clears his throat, those in hearing distance don't pay much attention, but when Judge Johns cleared his throat you knew he had something important to say. He was also real smart, so naturally we all paid close attention.

"It seems to me," he began, "that we want to find out which one of us has the smartest dog. The smartest dog, gents, not the fastest or the loudest, but the smartest. Intelligence, friends, is the true test of greatness." Judge Johns could always be counted on to get right to the heart of the matter. "So it seems to me," he continued after grasping his lapels and clearing his throat again, "that each dog ought to be judged on his reaction to a single command and the dog that reacts in the most intelligent manner will be considered the best dog in Doodenville."

We all thought about that for a while, and by and by it seemed fair enough. But then Digger said, "You know each man here might think that his dog done the best no matter what the other three dogs did. If that happens, it's a stalemate and we're right back where we were."

That sounded kind of correct. We knew we were all men of integrity, but we also knew each other and understood how sometimes a man's judgment could get clouded in an important matter like this one.

"Well," Judge Johns said after he cleared his throat again, "it seems to me we need an unbiased judge." You know, to this day, I get plumb amazed on how the Judge could always grasp things and have a solution so quickly.

The natural judge, of course, was Jessie. I say 'of course' because Jessie didn't have a dog. At least not since last spring when Old Clem Thurman's horses kicked Jessie's dog Cracker in the head.

Jessie agreed to act as the judge and took charge right away. "Since there are four of you," he said while grasping his suspenders judiciously, "one of you will have to go first and one will have to go last, and two of you will have to go in the middle, one ahead of the other."

I sat there and blinked because he had lost me at first. I didn't think that was possible because we always thought Jessie was a mite slow. He continued: "It seems to me we ought to go by age, starting with the youngest man. I will give you all five minutes to decide what you want your dogs to do." He fixed his one good eye on the clock that hung over the Buster Brown sign behind the counter.

After about three minutes and seventeen seconds I could tell everyone was done figuring what their dog was going to do. Steve snapped his fingers and smiled, Digger slapped one knee with both hands, and Judge Johns clutched his lapels and got that paternal courtroom smile on his face. Next to clearing his throat, he was famous for that. I had known right off what I was going to do. "Time's up!" said Jessie. "You first, Branson, you're youngest."

Steve sprang to his feet, snapped his fingers and said, "Bridge, get that dollar bill off Jessie's ceiling." Jessie had nailed a dollar bill to his ceiling years back because he said it was the first dollar he'd ever made.

After hearing his master's command, Bridge got up, shook himself off, took hold of an empty chair with his teeth and pulled it over to the potbellied stove. Then he looked at the dollar bill, back to the chair then moved it a little towards the counter. He did this procedure about three or four times.

Then before any of us except Steve knew what was happening, Bridge ran to the door of the store, opened it and ran outside. We couldn't tell how far he went because of all the blowing snow. It must not have been too far, because all of a sudden he raced back into the room, leaped on the chair, bounced at least ten feet to the ceiling, snatched the greenback with his teeth and did a perfect three point landing. I say three point because his left front leg kind of cracked like a stick. He was a mighty brave dog though, because he didn't even let out a whimper. Steve claimed later that it was because of Bridge's sensitivity to Jessie's wife's virus.

We all agreed that it was a mighty fine trick. Jessie pursed his lips and made a mark on a piece of paper. We all chuckled beneath our breath because we knew he couldn't write a lick, though he was obviously a good counter because he always seemed to know how many crackers we took from the barrel every Saturday night.

"Homer," Jessie called.

I was up. "Lock," I began, "go down to the jail and let Samuel Horn out and bring him here." Now, Lock had unlocked that jailhouse door a hundred times, I'll bet. I was always sort of afraid of getting myself locked in a jail cell accidentally, so I had taught Lock how to do it. I also knew that Lock knew who Samuel Horn was, because he was our best customer. Lock laid there by the potbellied stove and did not move. That didn't concern me because I figured Lock was just stretching internally or something. Pretty soon, however, it became apparent to me and everyone else that Lock wasn't going to do anything except move a little closer to the stove. I felt panic creep up in my throat and started to give the command again, when Jessie, with his thumbs around his suspenders, said very authoritatively, "Only one command, Homer!"

We all sat there in silence for about another minute and thirty-seven seconds waiting for Lock to get busy. But old Lock just laid there staring at the big iron stove and twitching his right hind leg occasionally.

I wanted to crawl under a chair. Everyone was stifling a smile except Steve, who was laughing his fool head off, and of course Jessie, who was keeping a Judge's face. I could really feel the blood boil and wanted to lash out and strike someone, preferably Steve. But after a certain age you just don't go around doing stuff like that. So I just sat there with all the humiliation and degradation of the world weighing me down.

"Your turn, Digger," Jessie said abruptly, since Digger was the next oldest or third youngest, depending on how you looked at it. Digger sat there for a few seconds, slapped his knee with both hands and stood up. "Spade," he said, (Digger was the assistant to the local undertaker) "...go outside and dig me a hole six feet by three feet and six inches deep."

Spade proceeded to do just that after he opened the door with his front paws and closed it with his hind ones. Showoff, I thought.

We all watched through the window as Spade braved the freezing weather and started his dig. We couldn't see him real good, though, because of the blowing snow. Digger claimed it was because the dog was moving so fast.

After about fifteen minutes, Spade came back in the store the same way he went out but in reverse. You could really tell Spade had been outside. One eyelid was frozen shut and he was shivering like mad from the top of his head to the tip of his tail. Plus there was frozen mucus hanging from his nose.

Before we knew what was happening, Jessie was outside with a tape measure inspecting the hole Spade had just dug. When Jessie came back in he was shaking almost as much as Spade. "If I got to make a decision," he chattered, "I got to know all the facts, right Judge?" The Judge did his paternal smile and nodded in agreement.

I was still feeling humiliated and had lost interest in the whole contest. No one was smiling or laughing at me anymore, but they didn't have to.

"Judge!"

"Yes, your honor." The Judge took a plug of tobacco from his vest pocket and took a big chaw. He just sat there for about one minute, chawing, smiling, and hanging on his lapels. Then without a word of any kind he tilted his head back and spat, in what Steve later figured was a forty-seven degree angle.

No more had the wad passed the Judge's front two silver teeth, than his dog, Bailiff, jumped up and ran for the spittoon Jessie kept at the end of the counter. Bailiff grabbed the brass bucket with his teeth and raced in the direction the wad was traveling and I'll be darned if he didn't jump four feet in the air catch the hulk on the fly right in the spittoon, landed not spilling a drop, and walked sort of nonchalantly, and perhaps a little arrogantly, back to where the spittoon was supposed to be and sat it down.

Jessie studied each dog, even mine, which I appreciated. He took a look at his "notes" and began. "Gentleman, after careful consideration and given the parameters of the charge given me I must conclude that that the most intelligent dog here tonight and therefore the best dog in Doodenville is …." He paused for the effect, then after clearing his throat and grasping his suspenders he continued: "… is Lock!" He slapped his hand on the counter.

"Lock!" We all shouted. I almost fell out of my chair. Digger did fall out of his, because when he went to slap his knee he missed and hit the floor. Branson started using powerful language and the Judge turned green, then red, then green again because he was halfway choking on his chaw.

Everyone in the room, except the Judge who was busy turning colors, demanded to know the reason for Jessie's verdict.

"Steven Branson," Jessie began. "That was a mighty fine trick, but look at Bridge's leg. It's going to take a good three weeks or so before it heals up and maybe not then. And Digger, Spade is shaking so much he'll probably come down with pneumonia or something, and Judge, you let Bailiff there put the most disgusting thing one could ever imagine in his mouth. No telling what he will come down with. Now the three of you made one command that I admit made for some powerful good tricks, but by doing so the dogs did not act very bright or intelligently.

"Now I want you boys to look outside. It must be eighteen degrees out there, and the wind's blowing a powerful lot. Now who in his right mind is going to go out there unless they had to? Yes sir, Lock is the best, the smartest, and most intelligent dog in Doodenville." And with the word Doodenville, Jessie brought the flat of his hand back down on the counter again.

I then said to Jessie so everyone could hear, "Your honor, give me a can of those dog biscuits and put a few more coals on the fire, I don't want a smart and valuable dog like Lock to catch a chill!"

Lock must have heard me mention his name because he opened one eye, took a deep breath, let out a pleasing sound of comfort and inched a little closer to the potbellied stove.

CHAPTER III

The Ballad of Clarence and Sally

Final Draft, as submitted to The Atlantic
by Homer I Storebeck

Dear Diary,

I met a man today. His name is Clarence Clam. Clarence does not come from around here. He says he comes from Alabama.

Just between you and me, diary, he looks like a scarecrow that lost some of his stuffing. But he is real cute anyway, and nice. Gosh, he's nicer than any of the men around here. I guess that's because he comes from the South. You know all those southerners are supposed to be real gentlemen.

The way I met him was like this: I was coming out of Jessie Miller's general store where I had bought some material from Mrs. Miller for half price. See, the store is going to close down and move to White Fawn, where life don't seem so demanding. Mr. Miller has told everybody that his wife's health is poor and she can't stand the rat race of a town like Doodenville anymore. She did look awful bad when I bought the material.

Anyway, as I was coming out of the store, Seth Rose bumped into me and made me drop my material.

I told him to pick it up and he said he wouldn't pick up nothing for a hog bellied sow like me. Well, that kind of hurt my feelings. I know I am a little heavy but he didn't have to remind me.

Well, not only did I get my feelings hurt, I got a little mad too, and started calling him a few names, when Clarence walked up and asked me if he could be of assistance.

Well, after seeing how skinny Clarence was and how beefy and mean Seth was, I told Clarence that he need not bother. Seth started laughing and walked down the street making sounds like a pig.

Clarence looked puzzled, and as I bent down to pick up my material, I started crying. Clarence bent down to help me and just as I was rising up, we hit our heads together. Well, Clarence being so skinny and me being a little heavy and all, Clarence fell backwards right off the planks into the street. I was so embarrassed I burst out crying again.

Clarence was a real gentleman. He got up like nothing had happened and introduced himself and offered me a ride home in his buggy. Now I have been raised proper and all, but no one has ever offered me a ride home before. In fact, no one has ever offered to do anything for me since Pa and Ma died.

On the way to my place Clarence asked me to move a little closer to him. Well, needless to say I was very upset that a mere stranger would be so forward and I was ready to get out and walk. But then I realized that the buggy was catawampus, and catawampus on my side.

Dear Clarence was just trying to make the

distribution of weight more even so his buggy wouldn't turn over. But he was too nice to call this to my attention. I moved over towards him.

I would never tell anyone this but while sitting next to Clarence with our legs touching, this strange sensation came over me. It made me all tingly. I never wanted the ride to end. But it did.

When we got to my place I invited Clarence in for tea but he declined, saying it wouldn't be proper since we did not know each other that well, and besides he had work to do. Well, I guess he could tell how bad I felt because he said he had really enjoyed my company and would deem it a great honor if I'd attend church with him this Sunday. I said yes.

Sunday is tomorrow and I wonder if he is really going to come by. I hope so. Good night, diary.

Dear Diary,

After church, Clarence and I were on our way back to my place, just exchanging pleasantries about the weather and all, when he said he hadn't been on a picnic since he came to the county. I asked him if he would like to go on one next Saturday and to my surprise, he said yes.

He picked me up in the morning and I had chicken, pickles, cheese, and some soft drinks all ready. We drove down to Arrow's Point that overlooks Lake River near Crisp Water Landing. We ate and talked all morning and around noon we ate again. We were halfway though the second jar of pickles and the third chicken when we saw Seth Rose and some of his ruffians getting out of a wagon down near the Landing. They didn't know we were there, which was fine by me.

They had a rope and some containers of kerosene and what looked like about ten cats. They were drunk of course, and very noisy, and used language that made both Clarence and me blush.

Seth stretched a rope between two trees and then took two cats and tied a bit of rope to their hind legs. He then proceeded to throw the cats over the rope so that each cat hung opposite from one another.

The two cats howled, bit, and scratched each other to death. Seth and his bunch just laughed and laughed. They did it twice more. Then one of the fellows doused the remaining four cats with kerosene and tied them together in the same way, but instead of tossing them over the rope, they poured kerosene in a circle around the cats and set the circle afire. The cats were scared to death and tried to run out of the circle, but every time one would break loose and try they caught fire. The hooligans thought this was funnier than the rope thing.

They eventually rode off, laughing all the way.

I told Clarence that was the most terrible thing I had ever seen and started crying. I must have cried for fifteen minutes. When I finally looked up, I saw Clarence was gone.

The buggy was still there, so I figured there was a good reason for his absence and then I noticed him down on the Landing digging holes. I watched him dig ten holes and bury ten cats.

On the way home we stopped for just a minute under an old oak tree and he turned to me and said, "I love you." I started to cry again but I did manage to blubber out that I loved him too.

He said he had something important to ask me tomorrow but he had some business to take care of tonight. I think I know what he is going to ask, or at least I hope I know. I hope also he don't get struck my lightning or anything. Good night, diary.

Wedding Announcement

Sally Withers announced the wedding of herself and the local town hero, Clarence Clam, who will soon be honored with a monument and plaque in the town square.

Sally has lived in the county all her life and is the daughter of the late Mr. and Mrs. Withers who were struck by lightning a few years back on their way to church.

Mr. Clam is originally from Alabama but has worked as assistant dog catcher for the last few months.

Mr. Clam and Sally will make their home in the Kansas City area, where he has accepted a position with the Humane Society.

Mr. Clam stated to this reporter, "I want to thank the county for the honor they are going to bestow on me and I am sorry I can't be here for the unveiling ceremony."

We would like to wish Clarence and Sally good luck and thank Clarence especially for his efforts in getting rid of undesirable elements.

Special Announcement

In conjunction with the newly formed County Literary Society, the County Caller has agreed to publish from time to time works of local citizens that are of a literary nature—meaning what is written, not the person, although I guess it could be one and the same.

The only criteria is that all submissions must describe local life true to the actual event described or close to it.

- Editor

Clarence Clam
By Homer I Storebeck

It was Saturday night, the night of the fight
When Clarence would fight big Seth.
The whole town was there to watch in the square,
'Cause the two men would fight to the death.

Seth was a bully and very unruly
And the Sheriff would turn all lazy
When he'd get a call from Dina's Hall
That Seth was going crazy.

Everyone was scared and no one dared
To challenge the crazy man
Who'd get his kicks from cracking sticks
Over someone's trembling hand.

But killing cats, (Seth was good at that)
Finally made one man rage:
"Who could be so mean to put kerosene
On a cat and set it ablaze?"

Clarence Clam was from Alabam.
He was tall and skinny and nervous.
But no one knew that because of a fool,
Clarence was gaining a purpose.

Did you ever sit, just quietly sit,
And wonder who you are?
And then begin to do your thing
And try to go real far?

I mean as far as you could, and hope you would
Become somebody great?
Clarence Clam from Alabam
Was going to have his day.

Seth hit Clam hard, and he fell in the yard
Of the house of the widow Tillie
And everyone said they thought he was dead
But then he started acting real silly.

Up he jumped and bit Seth's rump
Then started to gnaw on his leg.
Seth started to yell 'cause it hurt pell mell
Like Seth had just laid an egg.

Seth was seething from Clarence's teething
And Seth tried to run for cover
But Clarence kept biting faster than lightning
Looking just like a beaver's mother.

Seth kept fighting and Clarence kept biting
Then Seth began to groan,
'cause with one final bite with all of his might
Clarence bit through to the bone.

Seth was reeling, I mean really squealing
And really bleeding bad
And Clarence the Thin wore a big grin
You knew he felt awful glad.

Seth left town and went on down
To Manchester after that
And he never again did the hateful thing
Of setting fire to cats.

Now in the town square there's a monument there
And these words are on the plaque:
"To Clarence Clam, a brave, brave man
who's a protector of the Cat."

Dear Homer,

Again you have come up with a couple of winners. I liked the contest part of "Everybody Loves a Winner" and the way you used the poem to describe events of it, and "The Ballad of Clarence and Sally" was certainly unique. Unfortunately we can't use either of the stories right now but will put it in our Pull Pending File for later use.

Thanks again for your interest in The Atlantic .

Sincerely,

P.T. Sanders

PS: How did you come by Sally's diary?

Chapter IV

Everybody Loves a Winner

Final Draft as submitted to The Atlantic
By Homer I Storebeck

When Homer Chester moved from the county, he left behind a horse. Now this wasn't your normal or common everyday horse like all the others around here —it was a great horse. People in these parts had never seen a prettier or bigger horse than Homer C's (people used to call him Homer C as not to confuse him with Homer the Jailer).

No one ever quite knew the particulars surrounding Homer C's acquisition of the honey colored, seventeen-hands stallion called Navue. He did tell folks, however, that the horse was given to him by a bearded fellow in St. Louis, where Homer C was visiting his uncle. The bearded guy, who Homer C said must have been a real ladies' man because all the women that followed him everywhere he went, not only gave Homer C the horse because of a favor that was never really made clear, but left Homer C with a charge:

"Call the horse 'Navue', from now 'till the end of time, 'cause if you don't, the curse will get you with rope and lime."

Like people most places, Homer C did not put much store in a curse, but no one around here wanted to be wrong, so almost no one called the horse anything but Navue. But there is always one, you know, and this one was named Benny Pummel. Benny used to call Navue 'Honey.' "Ah, it's a honey of a horse," Benny used to say, and since he was naturally obstinate, he called Navue Honey.

When Homer C left for Kansas City, he could have sold Navue for what, in these parts, would have been a considerable sum. But he didn't. He gave Navue away, more or less. I say more or less because he didn't give Navue away as one usually thinks of giving something away.

Homer C was in a bind. He didn't sell Navue because he had gotten him free, more or less, and he didn't think it fair to make money on an arrangement like that. He couldn't give it away because whoever didn't get it would get their feelings hurt and he wanted to leave the county under the best possible circumstances. So after considerable discussions with friends and family, he decided the best thing he could do was to establish a contest, with Navue as the prize.

Great, a contest! That would make things fair enough. But what kind of contest? If you picked one kind it might show favoritism to a particular person who had that particular skill and there was always somebody that was better than someone else at something. So you can see what the fair minded Homer C was up against.

People tried to help and one suggested a foot race, but upon reflection, folks realized Crazy Jimmy Twofoot's oldest boy, Jimmy J, would win hands down.

Another came up with an oddball idea by any standard about a hole-digging contest. But then the oddball was reminded that Digger Johnson was the assistant undertaker, which gave him an edge.

What to do? Many tests of skill were brought up, but in each case someone thought of someone who would have an advantage. Folks did nothing but substantiate what Homer C thought in the first place. All things were rejected, rejected, and rejected again.

While walking late one night around town feeling sort of rejected himself, Homer C stopped in Jessie Miller's General Store to buy some coffee to perk him up.

"Hi, Jessie."

"Hi, Homer C."

"Hi, Judge, Homer, Digger, Steve."

"Hi, Homer C."

"Hi, Spade, Lock, Bridge, Bailiff."

"Bark."

"Jessie, would you give me a tin of Aunt Mame's and put it on my tab, please?"

"Sure would, just give me a minute while I hang these throwing ropes over my clock to get them out of the way. I really got took by that salesman from Kansas City. Seems like nobody uses throwing ropes in this county."

It was Saturday afternoon and the two finalists were Jimmy Reed and Benny Pummel. The crowd was ecstatic. Not only was a marvelous horse to be given as the first (and only) prize in the first (and last) annual Rope Throwing Contest, but also the two biggest rivals in the county were competing against each other.

Jimmy and Benny had been competing with each other in one way or another since their Pas, Jimmy Sr. and Benny Sr., had made a bet on whose kid would be born first. And ever since Benny Sr. collected his two dollars, Benny Jr. and Jimmy Jr. had been competitors. No matter what the contest was, folks in the county could count on two things: Benny (just plain Benny now, because his Pa died) would come in first and Jimmy (just plain Jimmy now, because his Pa died, too, but not until after Benny's) would come in second. Benny was used to winning and Jimmy was used to losing. Jimmy was tired of losing.

Two months before the contest, Jimmy bought a rope and began practicing. He did nothing else. No matter what time you would ride by the Reed farm, Jimmy would be out back behind the barn throwing that rope.

"Jimmy, you want to go hunting?"

"No, got to practice."

"Jimmy, you want to go dancing?"

"No, got to practice."

"Jimmy you want to go gigging, drinking, chasing?"

The answer would always be "No!"

Benny didn't practice as long as Jimmy. Why should he? Benny always won and Jimmy always lost. That's how things were. Benny bought his rope from Jessie's about a week or so before the contest and went out to his chicken farm and kept to himself until the morning of the scheduled event.

In the Saturday morning preliminaries, both men

went through the tricks that were made up by the Doodenville Men's Club, and both did them with ease. In fact, the skill, finesse, and dexterity displayed by Jimmy and Benny were indescribable, so I won't try.

The judges for the event were of course Judge Johns and "Judge" Jessie Miller: Judge Johns because of his experience in judging people and "Judge" Jessie because he sold the ropes at cost on the condition that he could be a judge, having gotten a taste of it the previous winter during the infamous "smartest dog" competition.

The afternoon event was "open." That is to say there were no prescribed tricks. Each man was to do his best trick and whoever had a trick the judges thought was the most stupendous would win Navue.

"Benny Pummel!" Judged Johns called out. "You're first."

Benny came strolling into the corral that was next to James Miller's (Jessie's brother's) livery stable. The crowd cheered and whistled. Everyone loves a winner.

Benny stood in the middle of the corral, grinning like he had already won Navue and had pocketed a ten dollar gold piece, which was a side bet he had made with Jimmy. He confidently waved to the crowd and they fed on one another's excitement. Gosh, how folks love a winner.

Benny signaled for the crowd to simmer down and they all hushed in anticipation. Then when Benny figured the excitement and tension had reached the right point, he let out a yell and Frank Pennington, the town half-wit, (technically speaking, Frank was not really a half-wit, but he did do some pretty dumb things now and then) came running into the middle of the corral with a chicken. He set the chicken down and ran out again.

While the chicken was strutting and clucking, as only chickens do, Benny began to twirl his rope over his head. He twirled it so fast that folks could only see a blur from Benny's shoulder upward. The town smith, Charlie Sauls, swore that the knot started to smolder like his tongs after an afternoon's work. Before folks realized what had happened, Benny had lassoed the chicken by the feet and through arm contortions and aerial distortion, he snapped the rope in a whip-like manner and had the fair fowl de-headed, de-feathered and de-gutted.

The gallery was stunned into silence. Benny brought the hapless hen back to the judge's stand and shouted in a demanding voice, "Bring me Honey!" Of course, he meant Navue.

The crowd began to scream and yell. Folks were so happy and excited that a riot almost broke out. Gosh, folks sure do love a winner.

Benny's feat was so fantastic and his voice so commanding that James Miller started to bring Navue (soon to be called Honey) out and present him right then and there. But, as in most emotional situations, cooler heads prevailed.

"No, now wait a minute," said Judge Johns.

"Hold on there," echoed Jessie.

"Rules are rules and they must be adhered to," Judge Johns said, grasping his lapels.

"Rules are rules, um, er, well…that's right, Judge," Jessie mumbled as he hung on his suspenders.

The crowd booed and hissed but Benny raised his hand to quiet them and boomed so all could hear, "They're right, friends. I'll get Honey soon enough." And the folks cheered. Folks just think a winner is the grandest thing.

"Here comes Jimmy," someone snickered, while others yawned.

Jimmy entered the arena with a rope and a bucket.

"What are you going to do Jimmy, rope yourself a drink of water?"

"That would sure be a winner!"

"Give up Jimmy!"

"Loser!"

Taunts were thrown in Jimmy's direction and everyone laughed. Everyone hates a loser, you know.

Jimmy was undaunted, however. He acted as though he hadn't heard a word.

Jimmy placed the bucket of water in the middle of the ring and stood beside it, his head bowed and his eyes closed. Some folks thought he was praying and others thought he was just concentrating, but everyone was chuckling.

After praying, concentrating or whatever, he swung the rope over his head and began to twirl it round and round. Around it went, faster and faster. The rope was moving so fast you could hear it kind of whistle. Just when the rope started to sing at the right pitch Jimmy kicked over the bucket.

Water came splashing out and along with the water came five of the biggest bull frogs I had ever seen, two of which had red ribbons tied around their necks, or at least where necks would have been if bull frogs had necks.

Faster and faster then the rope slung around. Then *zing*, the rope let fly and to this day I have never seen anything so amazing or indescribable in my life, but I will try to describe it.

The rope sailed in the general direction that the frogs began to hop. They were about ready to hop in five different directions and just when the quintuplets lifted off the ground, the rope grabbed two frogs by four legs and five frogs took off in four directions, with the red-ribbon frogs of course trailing the lasso.

Then in a single motion the rope once again whizzed around Jimmy's head, but with more vigor. Nothing but a blur could be seen. Jimmy was sweating, his neck was throbbing, and his every vein was bulging with pain. *Snap, crack*, and then another snap and crack. People turned to each other and wondered out loud what had been doing all the snapping and cracking. They were soon to find out.

Slowly the rope began to cease its frantic whirling until, at last, Jimmy stood there with his head bent, his chest heaving and bone weary right arm dangling a rope.

The crowd stared at Jimmy in silence. Then slowly, very slowly, with his left arm assisting his right one, he raised the rope over his head and at the end were skinned, white-meated, twitching frog legs ready for the frying pan.

Silence. Then, "Hooray!" The crowd exploded. People went wild. They jumped over and crawled under the fence and completely surrounded Jimmy. James Miller didn't wait for the judge's decision. He just wormed his way though the gathering with Navue and presented the stallion to Jimmy. The crowd cheered again.

"Unfair!" screamed Benny. "Honey is mine! Mine! Mine!" And with each succeeding "mine" Benny's voice went a little more hoarse. No one even heard or paid attention to him. Everyone was too busy hugging Jimmy and slapping him on the back and saying what a good rope thrower he was and that they had known he could do it all along. You see, everyone loves a winner.

Normally a story of this sort would end here. But remember the curse of rope and lime? The one the bearded guy told Homer C about?

Well, you remember how Benny used to call Navue 'Honey' and anyone that did that was going to have trouble? Remember?

Benny disappeared not long after the contest. It wasn't until many years later that Jimmy told me what had happened. Since the curse was given in a poem form, I guess it's only proper that you hear the results the same way.

The real story of Benny Pummell's disappearance can now be told because no one's around any more that it would much matter to. So turn the page to see how it goes. There is no title, so name it what you want:

Jimmy Reed had a gallant steed
That Benny Pummel wanted.
But a horse thief's life is not very nice
'Cause you're always sought and hunted.

One fine day Jim was on his way
To pick up the weekly mail,
When a rock slung out and hit Jim's snout
And he fell like a wounded quail.

When he awoke his clothes were soaked
And mud was all around.
He staggered to his knees and raged a plea
To track the horse thief down.

He went to the top of Old Mount Scott
To get a better view
And there he could see at ten and three
Ben and the horse Navue.

Ben was riding as free as can be
Among the mountains and hills,
Jimmy Reed saw and set his jaw,
"I'll lay that swine in swill."

Off Jim went, though weary and spent,
To catch the thieving scoundrel,
And swore he would catch the hood,
Whether by fair means or foul.

He tracked all night by the pale moonlight
Then nearby Potato Hill,
Young Jimmy Reed found his steed
And Pummel sleeping still.

Upon all fours, softer than snores
He crept 'till he was close beside.
Then he lunged for the throat and heard Ben snort,
And Ben's eyes he opened wide.

Jim took a noose from the Appaloose,
But then he changed his mind.
Ben's feet Jim tied to the saddle side
And wedged Ben's head 'tween lime.

Then he gave a thump to Navue's rump
And the horse took off at a gallop,
And if Benny could've he certainly would've
Agreed that he had fouled up.

Now some folks conjectured that Ben's in Fletcher
And others think South County,
But I'll tell you Mack, I know for a fact,
He's buried in both, you see.

CHAPTER V

Ezra Brown

Letter from Arnold Swift to Chester Murphy:

Dear Uncle Chester,

How is the family? Mine is fine.

Did you read about the murder in the Kansas City paper? You might have missed reading about it, since it's such a big city paper. So just in case you did or didn't here is what really happened.

Zeak Thurman was found dead about ten days ago down by Crisp Water Landing on Lake River. He was found by Steve Branson (that's Steve Branson the engineer, not the farmer. They are second cousins, however, but you know that, I guess).

When Steve came upon Zeak he just let him lie there because he was puffy and all. Steve, not Zeak. See, Steve had been hunting honey and found some, and he and the bees had a disagreement and Steve got the worst of the confrontation. Anyway, with those bee stings and all, it really swelled Steve up and when he found Zeak on his way home (Steve was going home, not Zeak of course), he couldn't hardly walk, let alone carry anyone anywhere.

Steve knew right away he had to get to the sheriff. Steve began sort of half running along the river bank towards Doodenville when the sheriff came riding up. Steve related what he had seen to the sheriff and told him where Zeak was. Since the sheriff couldn't do much for Zeak right then, he did take Steve over to Jimmy Reed's place, because Steve was in no condition to do much and needed some sort of medical attention.

While at Jimmy's, trying to figure out what sort of arrangements he was going to have to make to pick up Zeak and take care of Steve, the Thurman family rode up, led by none other than Old Man Clarence Thurman himself. First time Old Man Thurman had been off his farm in thirty years, some folks say.

Clarence said he had just found Zeak and was going to find Ezra Brown. You see Ezra had threatened to kill Zeak whenever he got out of jail. So naturally since the former had just gotten out, and the latter had just gotten dead, the Thurmans were looking for the former.

The sheriff told the boys to calm down, that there was no reason to believe Ezra had cut Zeak's belly open, but I suppose you remember how the Thurmans are: a real stubborn lot. They got it in their heads that Ezra had done it and that was proof enough for them. They rode off looking for Ezra after they had borrowed a rope from Jimmy Reed.

The sheriff hightailed it back to Doodenville to get a posse and Jimmy Reed took a wagon over to Crisp Water Landing to pick up Zeak. Everyone sort of forgot about Steve.

When the sheriff walked in the jailhouse he noticed Homer, the jailer, wasn't there. Homer's dog, Lock, however, was curled up around the stove, so the sheriff figured Homer wasn't too far away. And he wasn't – the sheriff heard Homer yelling from the back of the jail.

Homer had locked himself in one of the jail cells. The sheriff started yelling at Homer, telling him what an idiot he was, and Homer was yelling at Lock, telling him what a lazy dog he was, and during all this yelling about idiots and laziness, someone started yelling about loudness and not being able to sleep.

The sheriff looked in the next cell, and there was Ezra Brown, on his side with his front against the wall looking back over his shoulder.

The sheriff asked Homer what Ezra was doing there, and Homer said Ezra turned himself in for murdering Zeak Thurman.

The sheriff asked Ezra if he knew what was going to happen and Ezra said yes, he didn't care. He then asked Ezra why he'd done it, and Ezra said because he wanted to. Why, the sheriff asked, did he turn himself in? Ezra said he didn't have anyplace else to go.

The trial wasn't very eventful, what with Ezra's guilty plea. There is going to be a hanging in a couple of weeks. They have never done one in the county before, so everyone is kind of looking forward to it. If you haven't seen one, you might come down for the weekend.

Hey, I almost forgot. Have you seen Samuel Horn? He is up in that area now and I told him to look you up.

Well, give my best to Aunt Jane and Cousin Clara. See you later if not sooner.

—Arnold

Letter from Chester Murphy to Arnold Swift:

Dear Nephew,

It was nice to hear from you.

That is too bad about Zeak, but that Thurman family always was the type that would end up like that somehow or another. Too bad about Ezra, too, I guess. It really seems like he always had problems. Some people just don't get a break, or they make the Lord mad somehow.

We did hear from Samuel Horn. In fact he is going to come over and have dinner next Sunday. He is living in Independence. Says he has stopped drinking.

I am afraid we won't get down for the hanging, work and all. Besides I've seen one before. They ain't the most entertaining thing in the world.

Give my best to your Ma and Pa.

Write again,

—Uncle Chester

Death Notice

Ezra Brown died this afternoon due to a broken neck. He was the son of Miss Effie Brown, sole parent, not deceased. The events leading up to Mr. Brown's neck breaking are known by most everyone in the county and if by chance you don't know the circumstance, just ask somebody. It has been decided by the Judge and the sheriff that there will never be a hanging again in the county, "At least not while I'm Judge," stated Judge Johns.

CHAPTER VI

Swamp Gas

You can't get people to talk about it much. When you mention it, folks either change the subject or they just walk away. Sometimes if you come upon a couple of real close friends you catch an inkling of it, but the whispers end when they notice you.

Late one Sunday evening in June, folks in town noticed that there was a light on the southern slope of Mount Scott. After discussing the matter among ourselves we decided it was a campfire. We thought it strange, however, that the campers never came through town. You see, Main Street is the only way you can get to Mount Scott unless you can fly. No one gave it further thought, however, after they realized that Frank Pennington had been on town patrol and had probably fallen asleep while on duty like he always did. That being the case, it would have not have been that much of a problem for the campers to pass through without being noticed. We were not really surprised that they didn't let anyone know they were there. They must have been wanting to be left alone or they would not have picked such a desolate site to camp out.

The following Wednesday, while coming out of the church service, Steve Branson, the engineer, said, "Well

I'll be! Look!" We all looked in the general direction he was pointing, which happened to be in the general direction of Mount Scott, and we all noticed that the light from the campfire had moved from the southern slope to the northern slope of Mount Scott. We were just as astounded as Steve was, because we all knew that there was nowhere to camp on the northern slope, it was too rough and steep. Mount Scott, you see, is shaped like a triangle, with the northern slope being the perpendicular.

We were all muttering to each other about how strange it was when the campfire began to move across the face of Mount Scott back to where it had been before!

Well, that really made us curious, but not half as curious as when the campfire began to move up the slope towards the peak. That really dumbfounded us, but we were more dumbfounded when the campfire reached the peak and kept on going: not going back down the north part, but up, up, and up, into the sky.

I was shocked, the Widow Tillie fainted, and there were a lot of oohs, ahhs, gasps and shrieks. Someone started praying about it being the end of the world, and others just stood there like me with mouths open, staring in disbelief.

The light (we began to realize it wasn't a campfire) just hung in mid-air for awhile while we were all busy fainting, gasping, shrieking, or mumbling prayers. After a few minutes the light sat back down on the peak, stayed there for a moment and then ventured back down the southern slope where it had been before.

"It's a sign!" yelled Preacher Bob.

"Of what?" someone in the crowd shouted.

"I don't know, but it surely must be a sign."

C.O. Thomas, the only veteran we had in town, suggested that a bunch of us men arm ourselves and go up to Mount Scott and investigate. "I'm going to go up there and reconnoiter the situation so I need about twenty volunteers."

Well, that was out of the question, of course. I say 'of course' because you couldn't have gotten twenty men in Doodenville or the whole county, let alone those standing in front of the church, to go anywhere with C.O. But that did not seem to hinder him any—he, like many military commanders, thought that the troops were just as gung ho as he.

So brandishing his pistol, C.O. said, "Follow me, men!" And off he went towards Mount Scott. The twenty volunteers called for ended up being about six, and us six only went to try to talk C.O. out of the matter, or at least into waiting until daylight. But like with most commanders, the suggestions of his subordinates went ignored. Unlike most commanders, he didn't say anything about the quart bottles of whiskey Jimmy J. Twofoot and Frank Pennington brought along to fortify our courage.

It took about twenty minutes to get to the base of Mount Scott and we faced about another thirty minute climb to where the light was. At first we walked single file up the mountain path, and we obliged as long as C.O. was in front. Then about halfway there, we leapfrogged like C.O. instructed until we came to the point where we could see a glow from around the bend. Somehow, C.O. had managed to be the last one in the column and when we told him the light was just around the bend, he came up to the front to have a look.

After observing the situation—which wasn't much to observe—C.O. said, "On your bellies, men, and start crawling."

"I ain't going to crawl nowhere," Jimmy J. Twofoot protested.

"That's insubordination, troop," C.O. barked in a whisper.

"Come on Jimmy J, for Pete's sake, let's hurry and get this over with," said Digger Johnson.

"Humor the old ...." said somebody.

"No one's got to humor me! On your belly, Private Twofoot!"

"Come on, Jimmy." I always had a way with him.

A few seconds of tension passed, and then all seven of us got our bellies and began crawling closer and closer to the light, the source of which was still out of sight.

As we rounded the bend, however, we saw it.

We gazed upon a bright, yellow cigar-shaped thing in the clearing. It must have been fifty feet long. On top of the cigar there was a platform of sorts. We laid there dumbstruck, not knowing what to think or do. We really didn't have that much time to think or do anything because all of a sudden three man-like things just materialized on top of the flat part of the cigar. They were as bright and yellow as the cigar.

Two of the "men" bent down like they were working on something and the other was acting like he was supervising. We really weren't close enough to get a good look at them and the glow that radiated from them made their outlines a little fuzzy.

For some reason—to this day I'm still not sure why—we all stood up and just fixed our eyes on the creatures. When we did, the head yellow fellow seemed to notice us. No one was able to move due to fright and shock. No one in the crowd knew what we were looking at exactly, and no one really wanted to know, I suspect. We all wanted to leave, and fast. When the yellow fellow raised his hand over his head, that is all it took. We turned and tried to bolt down the hill, but we couldn't. No matter how hard we tried we couldn't get our legs to move! We struggled, twisting and turning and going though all sorts of bodily contortions imaginable. C.O., in desperation, drew his pistol and twisted from the waist so as to get a shot off towards the object. Well, he didn't have time to pull the trigger. The main yellow fellow pointed a small tube at us and a green light squirted out with a flash, and C.O.'s Civil War special was gone. It just disappeared.

We all stopped struggling then, closed our eyes, hunched our shoulders and waited for the green flash to make us disappear.

I am not sure how long we stayed in that position, but I eventually peeked out of one eye and saw that the cigar and yellow fellows were gone. "Can anyone move?" I asked out of the corner of my mouth. One by one the group opened their eyes, then as a bunch we started running, arms and legs flailing and whiskey bottles breaking, getting the stuff all over everyone.

We didn't stop running until we reached the front of the church, where everyone was waiting. We all started chattering at once, trying to explain what we had seen, but after Preacher Bob came close and sniffed us, he openly accused us of being drunk. The rest of the crowd got a whiff of our whiskey-soaked clothes and just knew we had visited Charlie Williams's secret still, which wasn't so secret, located near the base of Mount Scott.

"No!"we protested, but they insisted we were drunk.

"And besides," Preacher Bob began, "Judge Johns said that he had heard about things like those lights. They got one near Seneca and Joplin. It's just plain ol' swamp gas." And he went on to say that anybody who believed otherwise was either a drunk, simple minded, or a liar.

"No," I protested. "We know what we seen. Ain't that right, guys? Guys?"

A silence had fallen over our group. "Guys?"

No one spoke, they just sort of hung their heads.

"Well, I guess it could have been swamp gas," Steve Branson choked out.

"Yes I think so," chimed in Digger.

Frank Pennington and Jimmy J agreed with me, but of all the people in Doodenville, these were the two that you didn't want to agree with you. They both went on to describe the monsters they had seen up on the top and the yellow fellows suddenly had four heads and three eyes and spit fire. "I've seen them plenty of times, so I know it's the truth," came a shout from behind us. It was Charlie Williams, who was just stumbling into town, and as usual he really was drunk.

I was sunk. After Jimmy J, Frank, and now Charlie agreed with me, the whole town was laughing. These were not the folks who you wanted on your side.

One by one, our little group of seven seemed to float to the other side and laughed at the remaining, six, then five, until I was the only one left.

With the whole town laughing at me, I began to wonder if maybe it was swamp gas. Maybe those yellow fellows and the cigar were nothing but swamp gas swirled around with liquid courage. I didn't really remember drinking anything, but I've been there before.

To this day, I can't talk about it to anyone, not even the original seven. They claim it was swamp gas also. They say it's logical and it would not be the first time Charlie Williams' still made a man's head funny.

I don't want to be thought of as simple minded or a liar; a drunk is OK I guess, now and then, so when the subject is hinted at, I just wink and agree, "Yeah, swamp gas."

I do wish I could talk it over with someone because since that night I've come to realize one problem with the swamp gas theory. There ain't no swamps in this county, especially on top of a hill.

Dear Homer,

Great Job on "Swamp Gas". Sort of out of our vogue, I'll put in the Pull Pending File though just in case. Now, did you make this one up? If not, what was it?

PTS

CHAPTER VII

Old Horse, or the Story of Jerry and Betty

Horses don't lie down. I mean how many times have you seen a horse lie down, unless it was at the circus or in a painting? Old George told me once that he saw a horse lie down, but Old George lies a lot, everyone knows that. Preacher Bob said that he knew for a fact that horses didn't lie down and everyone knows he always tells the truth, or at least about as often as any other man. So I can say with certainty that horses don't lie down, unless they are dead, of course. This is a fact, and one you must believe, or much of what follows makes no sense at all.

Jerry and Betty Sonderegger were the most important people in the county a few years back. They were not rich but most truly important people aren't. They just did what they did and because they did it well, they helped our county grow and be somewhat prosperous back then.

You see, before the days of ice boxes or what are known now as refrigerators, the Sondereggers provided all of us in Doodenville with ice. Jerry said he got tired of warm beer in the summer and Betty didn't like her whiskey warm either, and both thought it uncivilized that anyone else had to suffer the same. That is when the idea came up to supply the town with ice.

Jerry and Betty were young when the idea first occurred to Betty. Jerry was looking for a job, and Betty was looking for Jerry most of the time. As most women, Betty had all the ideas in the family, and like most women, she concocted a means by which Jerry thought they were his.

Jerry, one day, inspired after Betty planted a seed, went out and built a wagon out of discarded wood and other junk he found around the county. It was a good wagon. Jerry was good at building stuff, but Betty grasped the problem right away and out of fear, planted another seed. Inspired, Jerry came up with another idea: "We need a horse, Betty."

Betty was glad her seed had taken hold quickly, because her fear was that Jerry would want her to pull the wagon. So Jerry went out and got a horse named Old Horse, which it was. Betty never gave Jerry much credit for being real smart about much, but she was astounded that he was not only able to get a horse so soon but with six months of feed thrown in, to boot. The whole thing, Jerry said, cost almost nothing, which was true because they had almost nothing—no money, at least—and Jerry told her not to worry about it. So she didn't.

With a homemade wagon, an old horse, and an old outbuilding, and it being winter, Betty figured that they could take the wagon up to the top of old Mount Scott, where there was plenty of ice coming out of the spring, and load up enough to get them through the summer.

No more warm whiskey or beer.

The first trip was successful enough that they filled up the outbuilding and felt real proud of their efforts. Now they had a homemade wagon, an old horse, an outbuilding full of ice, and two blocks still in the wagon which Jerry, to Betty's astonishment, promptly took over to Doc Walsh's. He was the one who sold Old Horse to Jerry for almost nothing. That "almost nothing," Betty figured, was the ice. Doc Walsh got tired of drinking warm alcoholic beverages, in his case, Scotch. Jerry, Betty thought, wasn't real smart but he must be pretty shrewd. Women always misjudge their men, except when they need them.

Jerry was content, but Betty saw a potential opportunity. She reasoned that if Doc Walsh would give Jerry Old Horse for two blocks of ice, then there were a bunch of others that might be willing to do the same. Not that they needed any more horses, but folks might be willing to trade something or better yet, pay money, which was a long shot.

Betty subtly mentioned the matter and Jerry said it wouldn't work and it wasn't a new idea at all. Jerry said they had done the same thing in Chicago, and said you needed a big storage shed or something like it, and a bunch of sawdust and other stuff, but he wasn't real clear what the other stuff might be. "It can't be done here," Jerry said, which was the final statement of most men when they either don't know the answer, or do know the answer and knowing it would just cause a lot of work that they were not really interested in doing.

But women usually don't know that things can't be done and so she figured out the solution. She knew that

Stan Blake liked to drink a little, and couldn't imagine that he liked to drink whatever he drank warm, and in fact heard him complain about it once during the town Fourth of July picnic. She also knew that he owned a large wooded area south of town and that Jerry could build anything he wanted if he wasn't content at the time the inspiration came.

"Jerry," Betty said one evening, "Stan Blake was complaining about having to drink hot beer next July 4th and said he would almost give anything to be drinking a cool one then, like you, I suppose."

"I guess Stan is going to be drinking a lot of warm beer then, because he ain't going to get any of mine," Jerry replied. "Don't have enough ice to share."

"You know, we might be able to trade him a half a block of ice for some firewood. We are running low," Betty said, almost absentmindedly. "He has all that wooded land just south of town and all he would have to do is clear it, sell the wood and plant a crop, buy a horse and wagon and he could have all the ice he wanted for his beer. You are sure right Jerry, everyone doesn't have the up and go-getting like you. I wonder what he would trade for, really, just talking you know, between you and me, I mean if we had enough ice ourselves, which we don't of course, and I don't see how we would get a bigger outbuilding. Most of the scrap wood around town is already gone due to the wagon."

"You know, that reminds me," Jerry said. "I haven't seen Stan for a quite awhile. Think I'll go on over to his place tomorrow and see what he's up to." And with that, Jerry went to bed.

It cost Jerry half of what was left of the ice, but in

two weeks, Jerry and Betty had a wagon, an old horse to pull it, a little larger outbuilding full of ice because of two more trips to Mount Scott, enough firewood for two winters, half of the crop that Stan said he would plant in the cleared field, enough cut wood to do something with if he ever had the notion, and what Jerry figured was enough ice to cool his and Stan's beer, Betty's whiskey, and free medical care by making a deal with Doc Walsh for ice to cool his Scotch. He didn't see why he would have to make another ice cutting trip until next winter. Jerry was content.

"Jerry," Betty said one day, "I was talking to Tom Roller the other day, and he said that he had felt kind of bad last summer when the widow Tillie died and they had to bury her due to the rot before her nephew could get here for the funeral. Said he never had that problem in the winter."

Two weeks later Tom the undertaker and Digger Johnson, his assistant, had a cold storage area to put bodies, Stan had a clear field and plenty of ice if he wanted it, and Jerry and Betty had a wagon, an old horse, half a crop, fire wood, free medical care and a free burial when the medical care was no longer needed. Plus, he still had a lot more ice in the out building that he had expanded, given an additional two more trips he made to Mount Scott. Jerry felt like he was set for life. He was content.

Betty, on the other hand, saw the bigger picture and with some seeding, Jerry began to realize that there must be a lot of people in Doodenville that might want ice for one thing or another and had something to trade or even a dollar or two. He would go up to

Mount Scott, get a load of ice, have Old Horse pull him through town and begin exchanging things for the ice. Most wanted ice and had something to trade, and to Jerry's amazement, some not only wanted some ice but also what others had given him in trade. Before you knew it Jerry and Betty were one of the most successful people in the whole county. Not that they had much money, but they had something more important: they were important. People began to depend on them and things just sort of had a domino effect.

Everyone was doing just fine. Jessie Miller started selling more alcohol, Doc Walsh had more customers, as did Tom Roller, and he kept his customers cold enough if need be. Digger made a deal with Tom to get paid by the hole, Stan Blake married the neighbor's daughter and let her kids from a former husband work the field and plant the crops, and the rest of the townsfolk had enough ice to keep their food cold, not to mention other things if need be.

But everything is a game, and games end. Jerry and Betty were getting tired and so was Old Horse. Jerry and Betty had come to love Old Horse, because they had spent a lot of time with him and they knew that he was the reason for their success. They would make one more trip up to Mount Scott, and then hand the business over to their nephew Kyle.

After loading up the ice, Jerry crawled up on the buckboard and gave Old Horse a little jostle on the reins. Old Horse turned around and looked at Jerry and Betty, took a look at the load of ice, then looked back down the hill and then just flopped over on his side and didn't move.

Jerry was puzzled and jumped off the wagon and bent down next to Old Horse to examine what had happened. After just a short while he stood and took off his hat. "He's dead, Betty. His heart must have given out."

"Jerry, don't you start crying, or you are going to make me cry."

"I know, I know, some might think he was just a horse, but he was our horse and more like a son to me than a horse, really."

"We have enough, we can trade or buy another horse for Kyle."

"Well that's true, Betty, but one thing you have forgotten—we got a wagonload of ice and no way to get it back to town!"

"We'll just unhitch Old Horse and pull it down ourselves," Betty said, trying to be practical.

"That won't work, Betty. The wagon is too heavy. We'd lose control of it and it would run right into town and spill the ice, damage the wagon, hit a building or two and maybe some innocent folks."

"Well, there must be a way," she said. "What if the wagon was empty?"

"Yes, but what would we do with the ice? I guess we could come back and get it somehow, but it would melt by then, I suppose, and what are we going to do with Old Horse? We just can't leave him here to be eaten by the critters. We can't bury him either, because the ground is too hard."

"Well just one thing at a time," Betty replied. "Why don't you walk back to town and get some help? We'll need it for whatever is decided, and perhaps one of us can come up with an idea by the time you return."

On his way into town, Jerry realized that he would have to be careful about who he asked for help because he didn't want the word to get around that the ice supply was in danger. If too many people got wind of such a thing, he feared panic would set in and foolish things occur. He had wanted a little time for the folks to be convinced that his nephew could take over the business. A new ice dealer and a new horse all at the same time might make people upset. He needed to talk to someone who would help him think straight, and when a man can't think straight he seems to only come up with foolish solutions.

Jerry decided that the two men he needed to see first were Doc Walsh and Tom Roller. They were pretty smart and would know what to do. Those two knew everyone in town on one side of their life or the other.

The three men talked in a conspiratorial way for a while and came up with a solution. Each knew two or three men that would help and could almost keep quiet about the matter, for a while at least, if they moved fast. Everyone was sworn to secrecy and would meet at midnight over at the funeral cold storage place at the edge of town next to the end of the road up Mount Scott.

Secrecy is a strange thing. You can always tell your closest friend, but everyone has a different closest friend.

Around midnight, twenty-five people showed up. Saws, spades, picks, and scoop shovels were passed out. The plan was unfolded to the group. All thought it was a good plan and set off up the hill to implement it, except for Digger Johnson, who stayed behind to dig a hole.

Betty was still sitting on top the wagon and everyone felt sad to see Old Horse lying dead.

Doc Walsh got things organized. Some of the men would saw the ice into thin slices and others would place them end to end on the ground all the way down Mount Scott to where the hole was being dug by Digger. It would be a slide for Old Horse when it was done. All they had to do was to cut Old Horse away from the wagon and let him slide down to the hole, fill in the dirt around him and then very carefully slide each ice slice down the same route and then store it in Roller's funeral cooler until it could be transferred to Jerry's place.

The ice would be saved, Old Horse would get a proper burial, and the wagon would be light enough to be pulled down the hill and not wreak havoc in the town.

After the slide was finished and assurances had been made that the hole was dug deep and wide enough, Jerry cut the reins holding Old Horse to the wagon. But before he did, he asked Preacher Bob to say a few words. Preacher Bob did, and Jerry cut the last leather strip holding Old Horse.

Old Horse started sliding town the ice when he suddenly opened his eyes, made a horse sound, and tried to stand up. His feet slipped on the ice and he couldn't get his balance and kept sliding towards the hole. Everyone began running after Old Horse. Some even slid on the ice after him, but to no avail. Old Horse finally managed to sit on his bottom with his squat hind legs and just seemed to watch the hole coming up faster and faster. When he reached the hole, he plummeted into the abyss, jumped back out, and ran though town down Main Street.

Old Horse was never seen again, so the people say.

Later, while sitting around the stove at Jessie Miller's, Doc Walsh said that sometimes ice and cold could bring animals back to life if, in fact, they were really dead. Everyone there agreed Old Horse had been dead, because horses just don't lie down.

Jerry and Betty bought two horses for Kyle to use, figuring one horse was just not enough, and Jerry altered the wagon as to allow for a two-horse setup.

The supply of ice was secured, Jerry was content, and for the first time in a long time Betty was too. She did keep suggesting things to her nephew, though.

I must admit that I was not a witness to most of the events just related. But I talked to enough people that were there, and all swear most of it is true, but all said there was just one troubling question that remained: Perhaps Old Horse wasn't dead (people began to doubt Doc Walsh's theory), and if he wasn't, why did Old Horse lie down, when horses don't lie down? No one but Old George ever saw a horse lie down. Old George told me not to complicate the situation. Perhaps Old Horse was just tired and wanted a little rest. Of course, Old George lies a lot. Preacher Bob, who never lies—I believe almost everything he tells me—summed it all up by patting his hand on his chest ever so lightly and saying, "It's a mystery."

Dear Homer,

Magnificent story about Old Horse. However, we don't really have space right now for your piece. We will put it into the Pull Pending File. By the way, what Doc Walsh mentioned is right about cold bringing things back to life. I have heard of that also. I am not so sure that horses don't lie down, however.

One more thing about the airplane story. It's good, but you do know that the county engineer was right, don't you?

Your Friend,

P.T. Sanders

CHAPTER VIII

The Pride of Doodenville Flying High

Almost nobody in these parts had even seen an airplane. So it was no wonder that when one landed in the middle of town everyone was real curious, amazed, skeptical, maybe even a little frightened.

Jimmy J was doing what Jimmy J did best, running. It was about noon, I think, when Jimmy J, while running down main street, noticed a strange-looking bird. Now Jimmy J is a mite slow, you see—not in running, in the mental process—but it didn't even take him very long to figure out what he was seeing wasn't just any old ordinary bird.

Jimmy J had always been taught by his pop, Crazy Jimmy, that when things don't seem quite right, or stuff is a little out of kilter, that you went and got help. And that is what Jimmy J did when he burst through the door of Jessie Miller's General Store.

"It's coming, it's coming!" he screamed.

"What's coming?" asked a startled Digger Johnson.

"I don't know, but it is almost here!" And with that he dove behind Jessie's counter.

"What is that kid talking about?" asked Steven Branson, the engineer.

We all just shrugged our shoulders and said we didn't know.

"Think we ought to go outside and look?" I asked.

"You know, I wouldn't put it past him just to do such a thing and then laugh at us when we got up to go see," said Jessie irritably. "Now get out from behind my counter, kid."

"Well, we all know," began Judge Johns after clearing his throat and grasping his lapels, "that Mr. Twofoot is a real fooler and he does conjure up more than most, but every man is entitled to be assumed innocent until proven guilty. We ought to go out and have a breath of fresh air anyway."

"You're right, Judge," snapped Steve.

"Well, let's go," echoed Jessie.

"Yep, let's go," chimed Digger.

We all sat there waiting for someone else to make the first move when we heard the most deafening, grinding noise any of us had ever heard before. The whole room shook. It sounded like a tornado or a rockslide ripping things apart, only worse. We bolted from the store into the street, so as not to be inside the place when the roof caved in, which we figured would be any second.

There must have been twenty or thirty people who'd heard and thought the same thing, because the street was full of people looking around and chattering excitedly to one another.

"Look!"

"Where?"

"Up there!"

And I'll be darned if this airplane, of all things, didn't come zooming down the middle of Main Street no more than ten feet off the ground. We all hit the dirt and laid flat on our bellies—everyone except Jimmy J, who ran as fast as he could in the opposite direction. Now we were not a village of giants, but people don't think too practically in stressful situations like when a plane is ten feet over your head.

An airplane with two sets of wings touched down at the end of Main Street and went up the road and over the hill out of sight. The crowd ran up to the top of the hill to see what had happened, but stopped short of descending the hill to where the plane was.

Judge Johns had read about airplanes so we all decided he should go talk to the guy who was just getting out of the flying machine. Judge Johns walked official-like towards the young man and we wondered what the two were talking about. In a matter of minutes the Judge motioned us to come on down. Everyone went, now that their fear had subsided.

The Judge introduced the pilot as Ted. Ted was a lean tall young man with fair skin and wavy brown hair. He was dressed in a brown leather cap that fit tight over his head with the ear flaps turned up. He had funny-looking glasses pushed back on his forehead and wore brown knee boots, a brown jacket with a deep brown fur collar turned up around his neck. From the top of his head to the tip of his boots he was dressed in some shade of brown, except for the dirty white scarf draped around his neck.

"Ted here," Judge Johns started telling the crowd, "has explained to me why he landed his plane the way he did, and I believe him. But I'll let him tell you himself."

"Thanks, your honor," Ted began sheepishly. He mounted the lower wing so he could get a better view of the crowd. "You see folks, I was about to run out of gas and it seemed like a pretty good idea to land somewhere. I was trying to find a place that was level and long enough to use as a runway and your road was the only place I could find. I'm sorry about the first buzzing down Main Street but I wanted you all to know I was coming so you would be sure to stay inside and out of the way of my landing. I really had to do some fast maneuvering, however, when I came back around and saw people all over the street." Ted searched the crowd with his eyes trying to find some sort of support, but all he was getting in return were blank looks.

I felt sort of sorry for him, so I decided to ease the tension a mite, and yelled out, "How much does one of those airplanes cost?"

Well, I suspect it wasn't the sort of question he was expecting, but he looked for the source and we made eye contact. "About seventy-five dollars, if you are willing to do some minor repairs yourself."

The crowd started murmuring among themselves. You see in those days, seventy-five dollars was a right considerable sum. It still is, of course, but not like it used to be.

"Why'd you land here?" Steven Branson asked.

"Well, like I said, I was running out of gas and needed to land somewhere and that happened to be here. I don't want to bother anyone though, I have a little money, so if you would let me buy some gasoline,

I'll fill her up and be on my way."

The whole crowd kind of chuckled a little and Ted turned to Judge Johns for an explanation. "Well, you see Ted, we don't have gasoline in this town."

Ted looked a little surprised and asked what we used in our cars and trucks.

The crowd's chuckling turned to hearty laughter. "We don't have any cars or trucks," someone called out. Then everyone started laughing real loud, even Ted.

"Whoops, my mistake," he said, and made a face that seemed to say "now what?"

"Listen, Ted," Clem Thurman yelled up, "I'm going over to Fletcher here in a little bit and I can pick some up and bring it back."

After some money exchanged hands, Clem left and Ted had some time to kill, as did the rest of us. Since this was the only airplane most everyone had ever seen or probably would, we were willing to kill the time with him.

We asked Ted about himself in general and airplanes in particular.

Ted said he came from a banking family in Chicago. His dad had wanted him to go into the family business, but Ted was an independent thinker and resisted. One day he was visiting the Cook County Summer Fair and he paid fifty cents for an airplane ride. He was hooked.

He joined the air show as an assistant mechanic-in-training and learned all about how airplanes operated. He saved his money and had one of the pilots teach him how to fly. He continued to save his money, eventually bought a fixer-upper and set off flying all over the country, earning his keep along the way by giving people airplane rides.

He had been almost everywhere. He had been to St. Paul, St. Louis, Indianapolis, Springfield, Illinois, and a hundred places in between.

We were all impressed. He said he was working his way to California.

Ted said that flying was like sliding on satin sheets towards a new adventure every time he took off. He said that when you land someplace, it's an end and a beginning, and that it wasn't the place you had been or were going that was important, it was the journey.

He went on to say, "Why, in just a few years there will be planes flying all over the country. There will be planes carrying people from Kansas City to Los Angeles. Some day men will cross the ocean in airplanes, and some day, in some sort of airplane, men will go to the moon and back."

Well, we all might not have been sophisticated city folks but we could tell that what he was saying had some powerful implications. We could accept flying all over the country in about fifty years or so, and may be even crossing the ocean in a hundred years, but the moon thing was just too much for most in the crowd.

"Now just one minute young fellow," Steve Branson challenged. "I happen to be the County Engineer and I know for a fact that flying to the moon is impossible. Why, in the National Geographic they just had an article about the moon and they say there ain't no air up there. So if there ain't no air up there how you going to breathe? Nope, ain't going to happen."

The entire crowd nodded their heads in

agreement.

"Well, I don't have all the answers of course, but some day it will happen," Ted said, "and we should not be afraid of new ideas. I know basic beliefs are hard to change and when they do change, people are fearful."

"What do you mean fearful?" Steve asked, slow and cool.

"Just what I said. Some people are afraid of losing the only way of life they have ever known. They criticized and berated Galileo, Copernicus, Columbus, and Darwin because they asked questions and sought answers and then drew conclusions about things others were to afraid to seek answers for, and were unwilling to accept what had always been taught."

Most of us had never heard about any of these guys Ted was talking about, but I did see Preacher Bob rubbing his chin seemingly trying to recall something when Darwin's name was mentioned.

"Boy, there ain't nothing in this whole county I fear, not even your crazy ideas." Steve replied firmly.

"Nothing?" Ted grinned.

"Nothing!" and Steve snapped his fingers and folded his arms.

Through all the years I had known Steve Branson, he had done things periodically that made me question his intelligence. This particular afternoon, it seemed, was going to be one of those times.

Everybody in the crowd knew what was coming next except poor old Steve. Even Jimmy J, who had wandered back in to town, had figured it out. Steve was too busy being obstinate and prideful to see it coming.

"I bet you are afraid to go for an airplane ride," Ted

said real quick, so as to draw out a quick response.

"I ain't either, I'll take an airplane…" and for a split second I thought Steve would turn green. He did turn noticeably white. He had gone too far and realized too late. There wasn't going to be any turning back. Steve Branson, self-appointed County Engineer, was going for an airplane ride. Steve sort of stumbled over and sat under the big black oak tree where Ezra Brown had been hanged, and if there had been a rope there, I suspect Steve would have hanged himself. I almost felt sorry for him—almost.

While waiting for Clem to return from Fletcher, Ted spent the time preparing the plane for takeoff and showing the rest of us some interesting things about the plane. At one point during the inspection, he took off the propeller and said so all could hear that if the prop goes, you have to jump and that is why you wear a parachute. "It breaks the fall so you won't break your neck. We used them all the time in the air shows and they usually work."

On the word 'usually' and the comment about the prop coming off, Steve Branson was beside himself. He had a hard time swallowing, and little beads of sweat popped out all over his forehead. He was near hysterical, and he was a stubborn man, but this might be the breaking point.

After Ted finished his pre-flight checks, he spent the rest of the time telling us all about some of his friends that had gotten killed in plane wrecks. He said that when he goes to meet his Maker, he wants it to be in an airplane.

When Clem finally arrived back with the gasoline,

Steve was almost hyper-ventilating and had to be helped to the airplane. "Now listen folks," Ted began (he had really taken charge of the situation), "you all have to stay off the road while I'm taking off and landing. I'm going to take off and land twice to check things out, and pick up and let off Mr. Branson, so make sure you all stay clear of the center of the road. Judge, could you and this gentleman (me) help get the crowd back?" We did.

"Now, safety regulations require that before I can take up a passenger who has never flown before I must do a P.P.C.O.R. Oh, excuse me, that's a pre-flight passenger check out ride. So I'll pick Mr. Branson up on the first landing. Because the checks are sort of technical, it'll take me about ten minutes once airborne, so have patience. To get a better angle for my landing, I'll have to fly around that big hill over there, dip in behind the peak, and then I'll be back to pick up my passenger. Now stand back, please."

The whole town obediently lined the road runway and watched as Ted cranked up the plane, taxied down the middle of town, turned and came reeling back faster than Jimmy Reed's horse Navue ever could have thought about. As he got to the top of the slope and where the road began a descent, the plane swooped up, up, and up.

He circled the town once, turned the plane upside down and flew it that way around the peak of Mount Scott. We waited for Ted to come around the northern slope but he didn't. We waited some more. Still no sign of Ted. Ten minutes passed, then fifteen. Every time, someone said aloud, "I wonder where he is?" or "is he coming back?"

Steve Branson would stir a little from his catatonic state until finally he was pacing up and down the center of the road shaking his fist in the air demanding that Ted return, ignoring all pleas to get out of the center of the runway so there wouldn't be any problems when he did.

Ted never did return, however. A lot of the town folks were mad at him, but I think I know why he didn't return. Ted was just a nice guy who didn't want to embarrass anyone. He had probably encountered men like Steve before and knew in the final analysis Steve wouldn't have gotten in the plane. Everyone needed to live a good portion of his life proud, and Steve, by not going for an airplane ride, would live the rest of his life as a kind of a hero in Doodenville.

And what about Ted? Well, I figured he would fly on to another town and then to another until he reached his destination, wherever that might be.

Several years ago I read about airplanes having "dog fights" in Europe during the Great War, and wondered if Ted was there. Then later I read about a guy who flew over the Atlantic Ocean all alone, just like Ted said someday someone would. And now at night, sitting on my front porch rocking the years away, I gaze at the moon and hear myself whisper, "Maybe, just maybe."

Epilogue

Several weeks went by before I received a notice from the Professor that he would like to talk to me about my submittal. I approached his office with a little internal trepidation.

"Mr. McAnally, I must say that your paper was unique," he said. "I normally look for more scholarly submissions, but since this is for undergraduate hours and the course is sort of new and unique itself, and since none of the other students did anything like it, I am going to give you the highest grade I can, which in this case is a B+. Now, off with you before I change my mind."

I thanked Professor Simpson and left immediately.

I made haste in running off to the old folks home. I zoomed down the hall, waved at Grandpa as I went by the door and heard him holler "Wait!" I yelled back: "Just a minute! I'll be right back!"

As I came to Homer's room, I opened the door to find an empty bed and a more or less empty room. As I was wondering where Homer was, a nurse came up behind me.

"You must be Mr. Storebeck's friend," she began. "I am sorry to tell you that he passed on last night. He thought you would come by eventually, and wanted me to give you this."

She handed me an envelope. I was sort of numb, so I opened it slowly, not knowing what would be inside. It was a letter.

The Atlantic
Dear Mr. Storebeck,

While reviewing our archives we came across an old Pull Pending File and reviewed the contents, many of which were yours. Our records are somewhat incomplete and there has been a lot of damage to certain portions of the submissions. However, yours, or at least the ones we have read so far, seem to fit a new section of our magazine that deals with the exciting new subject of village archaeology. We would like you to review all your submittals and resubmit them.

You have my assurances that they, with some minor editing, will be published in serial form at the standard rate paid for such.

We have had a difficult time tracking you down, but hope this letter finds you well.

Looking forward to hearing from you,

Yours Truly,
P.T. Sanders III

At the bottom of the letter Homer had scribbled in his rough handwriting, "send it in, boy!"

Who's Who in Doodenville

Editor's Note: The following entries should help the reader keep track of Doodenville's colorful residents and the relationships between them. Characters are listed alphabetically by last name. Characters without last names are inserted where appropriate.

Stan Blake

A somewhat uninspired farmer with too much woodland to clear, Stan's fondness for beer-cooling ice leads him to interesting trades, well-tilled land, and a marriage. We first meet him on page 67.

Steve Branson (The County Engineer)

Second cousin to Steve Branson, the Farmer. Branson (the engineer, not the farmer) is a prominent member of the community and is featured in more than one tale. He's admired for his knowledge but his pride sometimes puts his back against the wall. He's a member of the Doodenville Men's Club and is fond of his dog, Bridge, who is wounded in action in the course of our chronicle. Steve is first mentioned along with his second cousin on page 11, and we first see him in person on page 23.

Steve Branson (The Farmer)

Second cousin to Steve Branson, the Engineer. His barn was mostly burned down in an unfortunate incident involving Ezra Brown, Zeak Thurman and Samuel Horn—read all about it starting on page 11. He never appears but is frequently mentioned throughout the chronicle, mostly to distinguish him from his better-known cousin.

Miss Effie Brown

The sole parent of the infamous roustabout Ezra Brown, she is perhaps best known for being the only woman we know of in Doodenville to give birth out of wedlock. Ezra blames his life of crime on his fatherless status early in our chronicle, but Miss Brown is not mentioned by name until the sad events of page 53.

Ezra Brown

The infamous Barn Burner of Doodenville legend, Ezra is perhaps the rottenest of the town's few bad apples. It is not surprising that his misdeeds lead him to a bad end—one he faces with clarity. He first appears on page 11, and meets his fate in his eponymous tale on page 53.

Clarence Clam

Clarence Clam's tenure as a citizen of Doodenville was a short one, but in his brief time there he managed to find a wife and become a *bona fide* hero, with a monument in his honor erected in the town square. Little is known of Clarence's past, other than he is from Alabama and worked as as assistant dog catcher. He and his bride ultimately wind up in Kansas City. We first meet him on page 33, and he is immortalized in poetry by Homer I Storebeck on page 37.

Homer Chester

Known around town as Homer C to distinguish him from the better-known and more literary Homer I Sorebeck, Homer C leaves Doodenville for Kansas City soon after our chronicle begins. He affects our story primarily through his reputatation for fair-mindedness and his acquisition of the magnificent, but curse-laden, horse Navue. We first hear of Homer C in the tale beginning on page 41.

C.W. Flowers

The editor, publisher and reporter for the County Caller, the newspaper of record in the area. A fair and accurate observer for the most part, he was not above occasionally editorializing to sing the praises of a local hero or villify wrongdoers. Some newspaper clippings in his voice form part of the our chronicle. We first see his work on page 11.

Samuel Horn

One of Ezra Brown's cronies and partners in mischief, Samuel appears rarely in our chronicle. He is perhaps inordinately fond of hard drink, a habit which makes him a frequent guest at the local jail, which, in Samuel's words, is "sort of like home." While he is easily led to both trouble and the bottle, we see he is not completely irredeemable (at least in the opinion of Judge Johns) and in the course of our chronicle he manages to turn his life around. We first meet him on page 11.

Judge James Johns

A pillar of the community, the judge is commonly sought out for his wisdom by the townsfolk. We get a sense of the man from court transcripts and his moral choices about such dirverse topics as fair play and capital punishment. We also see Johns continue his judge role outside the courtroom as arbiter of various ill-conceived contests cooked up by the town's residents. An esteemed member of the Doodenville Men's Club, he is proud of his dog, Bailiff. Johns is first mentioned on page 11 and continues to be a major character throughout the chronicle.

Digger Johnson

Assistant to the local undertaker, Digger's chief responsibilities can be gleaned from his name. Digger is the third-youngest member of the Doodenville Men's Club, and is fond of his dog, Spade. Digger is known for slapping his hands on his knees when he is surprised or excited. He is one of the few brave souils to investigate the mysterious events described in the tale starting on page 56. We first meet Digger on page 23.

Sheriff Lenzi

Referred to only once by name in reporting from C.W. Flowers on page 11, he is otherwise known simply as "the sheriff" and features prominently in the unfortuate events described in the series of family letters beginning on page 43.

James Miller

Little information is given about James Miller, other than that he is the brother of Jessie Miller, owner of the General Store. James owns a livery stable, and the corral next door is the scene of one of Doodenville's most famous contests. James is first mentioned on page 45.

Jessie Miller

As the owner of the General Store, Jessie provides most of what Doodenville needs. He's got an eye for profit and even manages to turn seemingly worthless purchases into useful sale items. As the host of the Doodenville Men's Club, Jessie is happy to serve as an impartial arbiter of disputes when he is not keeping an eye on the level of the cracker barrel or the bottle of medicinal whiskey he keeps behind the counter. His dog, Cracker, was unfortunately unable to compete in the club's Smartest Dog contest. We first encounter Jessie on page 23, and see him show business acumen by seizing an opportunity in the tale beginning on page 41.

Mrs. Jessie Miller

The unseen wife of Jessie Miller, owner of the General Store, Mrs. Miller suffers from what is first referred to as "the virus," but it seems likely her disorder is nervous in nature. It will eventually lead her and her husband away from the hustle and bustle of Doodenville to White Fawn for more sedate environs. We first hear about Mrs. Miller on page 25.

Chester Murphy

Chester is not a resident of Doodenville, but makes his home in the Kansas City area. He is the frequent recipient of letters from his nephew Arnold Swift, who lives in Doodenville (though his responses to Arnold's letters indicate he is not as verbose as his nephew). We first hear about him on page 53.

Aunt Jane Murphy

The wife of Chester Murphy and aunt of voluminous letter-writer Arnold Swift, she is mentioned only once in passing on page 54.

Cousin Clara Murphy

The daughter of Chester Murphy and his wife Jane, Clara is the cousin of prolific letter-writer Arnold Swift. Her sole mention in our chronicle in on page 54.

Old George

We know very little of Old George, other than Homer I Storebeck reports that "Old George lies a lot." Old George's sole mention in our chronicle is on page 64—but who knows? The editor lies a lot.

Frank Pennington

Frank has the dubious distinction of being, in the politically incorrect jargon of the day, the "town half-wit." In truth, Frank's mental capacity is unimpaired—he just does a lot of stupid things. His brief appearance in the spotlight includes minor roles in the tales beginning on page 41 and page 56.

Preacher Bob

The pastor of Doodenville's sole (presumably Protestant) church, Preacher Bob is praised by Homer I Storebeck for his honesty. Preacher Bob puts down the strange events related in the tale beginning on page 56 as "swamp gas." He is not above prematurely eulogizing a horse on page 72. He is first mentioned on page 57.

Benny Pummel, Senior

The father of Benny Pummel, he dies prior to the beginning of our chronicle. He was the lifelong rival of Jimmy Reed, Senior. Their constant one-upsmanship is carried into the next generation by their sons. Benny Senior's sole mention in our tales is on page 44.

Benny Pummel

Widely known as a regular contest winner, the cocky Benny Pummel enjoys playing the perennial winner to Jimmy Reed's loser. A participant in Doodenville's first (and only) rope throwing contest, Benny is unhappy with the results and takes matters into his own hands, resulting in the tragic events described in verse on pages 50-51. We first meet Benny on page 44.

Jimmy Reed, Senior

The father of Jimmy Reed, he is deceased by the time our chronicle begins (losing his final contest with his lifelong rival Benny Pummel, Senior, who dies first. His rivalry with Benny Senior is mirrored in his son's constant competition with Benny Junior. We hear about Jimmy Senior for the first and last time on page 44.

Jimmy Reed

A good-natured hard worker, Jimmy Reed is nevertheless known as Doodenville's biggest loser. His lifelong (and mostly unsuccessful) rivalry with Benny Pummel, the town's biggest winner, is a legacy of the one-upsmanship between their fathers. Jimmy's dedication to practicing rope-throwing leads to his vindication, and his rivalry with Benny Pummel comes to an end in verse form on pages 50-51. He lends material assistance to Sheriff Lenzi on page 53, and he first appears on page 44.

Tom Roller

Tom Roller serves as Doodenville's undertaker, with the able assistance of Digger Johnson. In need of ice to keep corpses cool, he makes a trade with ice dealers Jerry and Betty Sonderegger. He is first mentioned on page 68.

Seth Rose

Like Ezra Brown, Seth Rose is one of the few truly bad apples in Doodenville. Described in Sally Withers' diary as "beefy and mean," Seth is rude to ladies and enjoys torturing cats with his band of ruffians. Eventually Seth gets his just desserts and relocates in shame to Manchester. We first meet him on page 33.

P.T. Sanders

While not a denizen of Doodenville, Sanders was one of the few outside the community to know what went on there. As editor of *The Atlantic*, he received numerous submissions from Homer I Storebeck. He published none of them, but this didn't stop the two men from striking up a friendship during the course of their correspondence. Though he never included Homer's stories in *The Atlantic*, he seems to have read them all and fulfilled his promise to put the stories in the Pull Pending file, leaving them for future editors to rediscover. Sanders is first encountered in a rejection letter on page 22.

P.T. Sanders III

A relation of P.T. Sanders (his grandson, we assume), he eventually takes ove the editorship of *The Atlantic*, and makes a decision Homer I Storebeck has long waited to hear - and in the nick of time. We meet him through his fateful correspondence on page 87.

Charlie Sauls

Mentioned only once in our chronicle, Charlie Sauls is Doodenville's resident blacksmith. He is featured (briefly) on page 46.

Betty Sonderegger

Betty Sonderegger is the wife of Doodenville's ice daler, Jerry, and may well be the power behind the throne of the family business, which she hopes to leave to her nephew, Kyle. Betty's chief contribution to the history and culture of Doodenville stems from the fact that she thinks it uncivilized to drink warm whiskey. She first appears along with her husband on page 64.

Jerry Sonderegger

Jerry Sonbderegger is described as one of the most important people in Doodenville—not for any particular wisdom or talent, but from his status as the sole perveyor of ice, which he brings down from Mount Scott with the stalwart aid of Old Horse. Good at building useful items out of junk, he is perhaps better at subconsciously taking advice from his wife, Betty. Jerry is the uncle of Kyle, who will eventually take over the family business. Jerry first appears along with his wife on page 64.

Kyle Sonderegger

The nephew of Jerry and Betty Sonderegger, he takes over the family business when his uncle and aunt retire. He is first mentioned on page 69.

Homer I Storebeck

Our chief source of the *Tales From Homer*. He served as Doodenville's city jailer, unofficial town historian and poet laureate. A frequent hopeful contributor to *The Atlantic* magazine, his stories chronicled the everyday lives and misadventures of Doodenville. Happily, he is finally vindicated as a writer after years of rejection slips. He first appears on page 8.

Arnold Swift

We know almost nothing about Arnold Swift, other than that he was seemingly a friend of Samuel Horn and that he carried on a voluminous correspondence with his uncle, Chester Murphy. These letters form the basis of the tale tat begins on page 52.

Ted, the Aviator

Ted is not a resident of Doodenville, and as far as we know, visited only once. Nevertheless, he looms large in local legend. He is adventurous and charming, a pursuer of freedom, and predicts great things for the future of manned flight. When given a chance to humiliate Steve Branson (the engineer, not the farmer), he shows his true quality, and leaves behind a legacy of dreams. We first meet him and his fantastic flying machine on page 77.

C.O. Thomas

The only veteran living in Doodenville, C.O. Thomas takes charge of the investigations in the tale starting on page 57. We don't know his age, but he is referred to as "old" by his hastily mustered militia, and given the nature of C.O.'s antique pistol, we can safely assume he is a veteran of the Civil War. He makes his entrance to our chronicle on page 58.

Clarence Thurman

Better known as Old Man Thurman, he is the nominal head of the Thurman clan, noteworthy for their stubborn nature and impulsiveness. He is the father of the helpful Clem Thurman and the hapless Zeak Thurman. Old Man Thurman, a notorious recluse, rarely leaves his farm, and does so in our chronicle as the leader of an enraged posse on page 53.

Clem Thurman

A member of the troublesome and impulsive Thurman clan, Clem seems a bit more civilized than his brother Zeke or his Old Man Clarence. One of his horses kicks dogs in the head, but otherwise we see him as the type of helpful neighbor who would drive to Fletcher to get gas for a stranger. It's unclear whether he joined the Thurman clan's quest for revenge against Ezra Pound. Clem is first mentioned on page 26 and plays a helpful role in the tale beginning on page 75.

Zeak Thurman

A member of the Thurman clan, Zeak was a one-time minion of the notorious county troublemaker, Ezra Brown. Perhaps Zeak had a touch of his brother Clem's good nature, for during the town's infamous "Barn Burner" episode, he finds his courage in the courtroom. Unfortunately, we find he pays a steep price for it. We first encounter Zeak on page 11, and learn of his ultimate fate in the tale beginning on page 53.

Widow Tillie

We know little of Widow Tillie, other than that she appears to have been an active churchgoer. She faints on page 57 and dies on page 68.

Crazy Jimmy Twofoot

A character-about-town, Jimmy's name comes from his weird dance frenzies and penchant for selling caramel apples during court proceedings. He has passed his eccentricities down to Jimmy J, his fleet-footed son. Crazy Jimmy first appears on page 13.

Jimmy J Twofoot

The "J" is presumably for "junior," as Jimmy J is the son of local character and sometime caramel apple salesman Crazy Jimmy Twofoot. Jimmy J isn't known for his intellectual gifts, but he is known as the fastest runner among all of Doodenville's citizens. He makes several appearances in our chronicle, helping to investigate the events described in the tale starting on page 56, and he is the first person in town to notice the aviator who visits in the final tale of our volume. Jimmy J is first mentioned on page 24.

Doc Walsh

Doodenville's only physician, Doc Walsh's practice does not seem much affected by his fondess for Scotch. His fondess for *cold* Scotch even leads him to trade medical care for ice. He once owned Old Horse, but sold the animal for "almost nothing," and goes on to play a part in the horse-related hijinks in the tale beginning on page 64. He first appears on page 66.

Charlie Williams

Charlie Williams is known to the folk of Doodenville as an irresponsible drunk, but this does not stop them from occasional visits to his not-so-secret still at the base of Mount Scott. It is likely he is directly related to the troubled J.T. Williams. He makes his first appearance, to Homer I Storebeck's consternation, on page 61.

J.T. Williams

Mentioned only once in our chronicle, we must presume Williams was declared insane and removed to the appropriate facility "up north." It is unclear whether he is related to moonshiner Charlie Williams, but in the tight-knit community of Doodenville, but it seems likely for a variety of reasons. J.T.'s lone mention is on page 15.

Sally Withers

Sweet-natured and heavy set, Sally was orphaned when her parents were struck by lightning on their way to church. Her life changes when she encounters Clarence Clam, who courts her in gentlemanly fashion and becomes the town hero. Sally was a faithful recorder of her life in her private diary, pages of which illuminate our tales, but it is unclear how our chronicler gained access to her diary. We first encounter Sally in her own voice on page 33.

Practical Jokers

An excerpt from *Tales From the Lake*
By Conley Stone McAnally

Charges were dropped against Jimmy Jay and Joseph See by Municipal Court Judge Homer Simms. Everyone around the Lake was relieved. No one could remember anyone living there who had ever spent time in jail. But given the recent antics, a spokesman for Judge Simms said that, as always, the judge would have no statement as to the ruling. However, the spokesman did say that sometimes charges are dropped when it is not clear what a person has been charged with.

It was no secret that Jimmy and Joseph were taken into custody after engaging in a brawl, or what appeared to be brawl, across the street from Jimmy's house. Witnesses said that when the two men were hauled off by authorities, both kept telling Deputy Sheriff Wilson that it was just a misunderstanding. The deputy said that most fights were, and took them to jail.

Jimmy and Joseph were good friends and brothers-in-law and no one living around the Lake could imagine them disagreeing to the degree whereby a brawl would be forthcoming.

Jimmy liked two things most of all. One was his hunting dog Killer, and the other was playing tricks on Joseph. Joseph liked two things. One was scrounging around the back exits of retail stores up in Dairymount collecting things discarded in the dumpsters, and the other was playing tricks on Jimmy. Their tricks or practical jokes they played on one another were legendary around the neighborhood.

It had been three weeks since "someone" put Limburger cheese on the manifold of the car owned by Joseph. Although neither of them ever admitted they were the ones playing tricks on each other, Joseph knew it was Jimmy. Jimmy knew that Joseph would do something in return but it seemed as though it was taking Joseph a little bit longer than normal to return the gesture. Waiting became a little unsettling for Jimmy.

One evening Joseph was scrounging around the back alley of the TG&Y up in Dairymount when he came across a female mannequin. It was in two parts, the bottom and the top. Joseph thought in it might look funny in the Lake stuck in mud with the head part on one side and the bottom half next two it with the legs in the air. While loading the two parts in the car he noticed an old hairpiece that must have at one time belonged to the manikin. He took it for good measure. On his way home a seed of an idea started to grow. The idea grew more every time he took a breath and whiffed Limburger cheese.

Joseph knew that Jimmy took his dog Killer to the junkyard down by the river every Friday after work. Killer would chase anything that ran along the riverbank. Jimmy told everyone that it was a good way for

Killer to keep his hunting instincts intact in case they ever went hunting. The neighbors appreciated Jimmy doing it so Killer would not get the urge to chase their cats or chickens some had in their back yards. Little did they know that their fear was unfounded and if ever there was a dog missed named it was Killer—miniature Dachshunds don't usually strike fear in the hearts of man or beast.

Jimmy's wife, Evelyn, never went with Jimmy and would usually go visit her sister, Joseph's wife, who lived just four doors down the street. Joseph, knowing this, thought a Friday would be an opportune time to implement his plan.

On the Friday selected, Joseph discovered Evelyn was on a diet and that she decided not to visit her sister. The newest member of the Ladies Auxiliary, Mrs. Hertzog, was going to bring some Romanian calzones for a treat that evening and Evelyn did not want to be tempted. At first, Joseph was disappointed until he learned that Evelyn decided to accompany Jimmy to the riverbank to see Killer in action.

Joseph saw an additional opportunity for a prank, and on his way out to perform what nonsense he had in mind, he stopped by Mrs. Hertzog's place to see if she would let him have a calzone because he said he was afraid none would be left when he got home after the meeting his wife was having that night. Mrs. Hertzog was flattered, of course, and gave him two. Joseph then set off towards Jimmy's house.

It was dark, there were no street lights, and he knew that Jimmy never locked his front door. No one saw him carry the mannequin inside the house.

He placed the top part of the mannequin in Jimmy and Evelyn's bed with only the head protruding. He then smeared some of the calzone on the top of the plastic head and put the wig over that. Under the bed he slipped the bottom torso so as only to expose the legs.

Joseph drove around the block and parked his car in his own driveway, took a folding chair from the garage, and walked back down towards Jimmy and Evelyn's place, and took up a position across the street behind a bush, unwrapped the other calzone and started eating it while he waited.

Joseph was about half way through his calzone when Jimmy, Evelyn, and Killer pulled into Jimmy's driveway. As soon as the door was opened, Evelyn jumped out of the car and ran inside because she had to use the bathroom. Killer immediately followed. As Jimmy was rounding the rear of the car he heard Killer growl and Evelyn scream. Jimmy dashed up the front porch steps and encountered Killer running out of the house with a mouth full of hair tainted with red. Killer ran up the street and while Jimmy was deciding whether to chase Killer or see if Evelyn was all right, Evelyn came running out of the house with a shawl over her head screaming and ran in the opposite direction from where Killer had gone.

Jimmy's first instinct was to run after Evelyn, but she was heading in the direction of her sister's, so he knew that she would be safe and, if necessary, receive proper medical attention. He thought that Killer had finally shown his true nature and pulled Evelyn's hair off to punish her for intruding on his time with his master.

Jimmy did not want to see Killer attack anyone else in a dog-frenzy, so he went after Killer to try and calm him down.

Killer finally stopped running about five houses up the street, but every time Jimmy would come close, Killer would run one direction then another, always carrying Evelyn's bloody head of hair. All of a sudden Killer stopped. He looked around, cocked his head and made a beeline towards the bush Joseph was sitting behind enjoying the whole show along with a number of neighbors who had congregated outside when they heard Evelyn screaming and Jimmy yelling at Killer.

Before Joseph could react, Killer jumped on Joseph's back. Apparently, it was decided later, Killer had smelled the calzone under the wig of the mannequinand tried to eat it, not realizing at first that the wig was only tainted with the calzone sauce and not edible. Having a good nose like all Dachshunds and all the excitement of Evelyn screaming and Jimmy chasing him, he smelled the calzone Joseph was eating and ran immediately for Joseph and knocked Joseph from his chair and grabbed for the calzone. Joseph was not about to give up his calzone so easily and started wrestling with Killer. Jimmy, having thought Killer had gone mad and attacking his friend, jumped into the fray and tried to separate Killer and Joseph. Killer managed to separate the calzone from Joseph's clutch and ran up the street out of sight. While laying there breathless, all Jimmy and Joseph could do was watch Killer dash away with the calzone and Evelyn's head of hair which, of course, belonged to the manikin.

As good or bad luck what would have it, depending on one's point of view, Deputy Sheriff Wilson came driving down the road and wondered why all the neighbors were outside surrounding a bush. He stopped the patrol car and saw Jimmy and Joseph laying over the top of one another, breathless. Jimmy said something about his wife being scalped and Joseph said that his calzone had got eaten, and Evelyn came wandering back with her sister Mary, yelling that there was a body in the house.

After making sure there wasn't really a body in the house, Deputy Sheriff Wilson decided to take the two down to the courthouse so he could sort the whole thing out after ensuring there wasn't really a real body in the house.

Judge Simms thought that the deputy was correct to bring the two in and let things calm down in the neighborhood, but did not see a crime Jimmy and Joseph could be charged with. Like he told Deputy Sheriff Wilson, "It ain't a crime to be stupid."

Jimmy and Joseph remained friends and promised each other, their respective wives, and Judge Simms that their practical joking days are were over. Joseph even put up half of the $10 reward for anyone who found and returned Killer. However, every April 1st for many years there after, folks wondered if the truce would hold.

Editor's note: You can purchase Tales From the Lake *by visiting www.pharaohpublishingusa.com or find it on* Amazon.

About the Author

Photo by Beverly McAnally

Conley Stone "Snapper" McAnally is a retired U.S. Army Reserve officer and public school teacher. He is a former columnist for *The Examiner* of Independence, Missouri, where he cataloged his experience as a teacher in "bush" Alaska among the Yupik and Inupaque Eskimos. Several of his observations have been published in *Whispering Wind*, a magazine about Native American life and culture. His blog, The Adventures of Conley McAnally, is at conleymcanally.blogspot.com. He is also the the author of several short stories and novellas. He is the father of five children and grand father of 15. He currently resides with his wife Beverly in Tucson, Arizona.

Pharaoh Publishing USA is an artisanal micropublisher of books, music and games in the Heart of America. We do not accept unsolicited materials.

Contact us at pharaohpublishingusa@gmail.com.